THE SECRET BEHIND THE BOOKCASE

A Jane Teaberry Mystery
Book 1

E. J. Garrett

Hundred Acre Press LLC
Cincinnati, Ohio

This book is dedicated to my daughters and
granddaughters.

CHAPTER ONE

THE BULLY

"TRY NOT TO lose this match, Jane. It's our last tennis match of the season, and you know how you are. Don't choke today or you'll be sorry," said Brandi Brown with a snarl. Brandi flipped her golden blonde hair over her shoulder and turned to strut down the hallway of West Midland High School with her two besties, Heather and Brittany.

Jane Teaberry's senior year had been pretty good, except when Brandi was tormenting her about something or another. She couldn't believe there was a time when she actually liked Brandi, and even thought they were friends. Brandi wasn't a better tennis player, so she couldn't understand why she acted the way she did since she became captain of their team.

Jane bristled at Brandi's comment, and with a quick turn of her head, she glared at Brandi. *What's that supposed to mean?* she thought to herself, as she kept walking.

"No problem, Brandi," responded Jane. She then pretended to smile with her best effort. She could feel her face getting red. Her body tensed and she even felt pain in her jaw. Jane loved playing tennis, but often wished she was on a different team.

Jane quickly turned away from the unpleasant trio. Dodging the oncoming clusters of students pouring out of a classroom, she rounded the corner toward the main hallway. The echoing sounds of multiple conversations and slamming lockers in the school hallway drowned out anything else Brandi may have said.

Jane was going to do the best she could, no matter whether Brandi supported her as a teammate, or threatened her with who knows what. She was tired of Brandi's bullying, but felt there was nothing she could do about it. She was almost at the end of her high school career, and she still hadn't figured out how to handle some of the most common teenage problems.

Jane sighed as she tried to shrug off Brandi's comment… again. She tried to ignore Brandi and her pals, but it wasn't easy. Playing tennis on a team required support from teammates, and Brandi seemed to have done her best to destroy the confidence of several members of the team, including Jane.

Jane stopped at her locker to drop off her books and grab her tennis gear. As she opened her locker and shoved her books onto the top shelf, Jane noticed a girl struggling to open her locker. "Do you need some help?" she asked.

"That would be great," said the girl. "I just moved here and still had to attend the last few weeks of school. It'll be over before I get the hang of this lock, and then they'll probably give me a different one next year. Here's the combination." She showed Jane a slip of paper.

"Hi, I'm Jane," said Jane, as she started working on opening the lock.

"I'm Eloise," said the girl.

"Here you go," Jane said, as she popped open the locker.

"Thank you so much!"

"Sorry but I'm in kind of a hurry," said Jane, as she stepped back over to her own locker and pulled out her tennis bag. She shut the locker and said, "Good luck, Eloise. And good luck next year, too."

"Thanks, Jane!" said Eloise.

Jane turned to look both ways behind her to make sure Brandi wasn't around, and then hoisted her heavy tennis bag over her left shoulder and headed toward the exit. When she pushed open the door and stepped out into the warm sun, the bright sky caused Jane to shield her eyes at first. She stopped for a moment, took a deep breath and scanned the landscape.

Breathing in the fresh air felt liberating in comparison to the stuffy air in the hallway of the school. The sky was bright blue, and the sun was partially hidden behind a few puffy clouds that resembled balls of cotton.

Jane could feel the warmth from the sun on her

cheeks and it made her smile. Something about the outdoors always made her feel better, and today's weather was perfect for being outside. Jane wondered at times whether her love for tennis was just an excuse to be outdoors.

The balmy temperature of 74 degrees seemed perfect for today's tennis match. Jane noticed a light breeze and wondered if the wind was going to be a factor in the match.

Her friend, Peaches Parker, was waiting for her outside the door. Peaches had been Jane's doubles partner all year, ever since she moved to West Midland from Florida. Peaches had an older brother, Thomas, who was overseas in the Marines, just like Jane's brother Michael. They shared a common bond over their brothers. Jane was comforted to have a friend who could understand how she felt about having a brother so far away, and not ever knowing if he was safe.

"We're on court five," said Peaches, as she picked up her tennis bag and turned to walk with Jane toward the West Midland High School tennis courts. The high school was built two years ago to combine two of the older county high schools into one large new one with modern amenities.

The six tennis courts were added last summer. They were enclosed with a high fence and connected to the school building via a paved pathway. Jane and Peaches and their team had enjoyed practicing and playing all of their home matches on the new courts all season.

"Mm, okay," said Jane, as they walked along the paved path out to the courts.

Peaches stopped in her tracks. "Um… hello… what's wrong?" she asked.

"Nothing," said Jane. "I'm a little nervous about the match today. I sure hope we win."

"We will," said Peaches. She looked at Jane. "You didn't happen to see our team captain on the way out here, did you?"

"I did see her in the hallway," said Jane. "I think she has no idea how she makes people feel. But I'm fine. I just want us to win today."

Peaches knew what Brandi might have said, as she was all-too familiar with her interactions with Jane and some of the girls on the team.

"O M G, Jane. I knew it! She's always messin' with your head. That girl wouldn't dare mess with me. I'd give her a stare-down that would make her pretty blonde hair stand on end. I don't know why they picked her for the captain," replied Peaches. "She's not captain-like."

"I did notice she never says anything to me when you're with me."

"Don't let her be in your head while we're on court. We can win this," said Peaches.

"I'm gonna to do everything I can to win today," Jane vowed.

"Good," replied Peaches, nodding her head. They continued walking out to court five.

Jane loved having Peaches for a partner. She admired her skills as a tennis player, but she also admired her enthusiasm and confidence as a person. She never had to wonder what Peaches was thinking, because Peaches was always open and direct with her thoughts.

When Brandi was Jane's doubles partner last year, they barely communicated on court and weren't in sync at all. Brandi didn't recognize any of the strategic shots that Jane had made, and didn't back her up when the opponent sent a lob over her head. Brandi assumed they were lucky shots when the opponent made errors that Jane had intended.

Luckily, Jane had been playing with Peaches as her partner all of this year. They had great communication on the court, and won at least half of their matches.

Jane and Peaches found their court and set their bags on the bench. They wore matching outfits in their school colors, black and orange. Peaches wore her curly black hair in long, tight braids. Today she had her braids pulled back into a large ponytail, so Jane had also braided her hair in a ponytail. They both tied an orange ribbon around their ponytails to present themselves as a unified team.

"I guess this is the last time we'll be wearing these outfits, now that our senior year is ending," said Peaches. "I kind of like them. I mean, they're kind of cute and all, but if I didn't have to wear school colors, I think I'd pick something else."

"I think those colors look great on you, with your dark hair and brown skin, but I agree, I would pick something else, too. They don't look good on me at all," agreed Jane, as she donned her court shoes.

"I don't know," Peaches pondered. She squinted her eyes at Jane. "You have dark hair, too. I think it looks okay on you. What color would you pick?"

"Maybe blue to match my eyes." Jane laughed. "I don't really know what would look good on me."

"Yeah, okay then," Peaches chuckled. "Your outfit doesn't have to match you, but whatever makes you happy, I guess."

"Hey, let's take a selfie, since it's our last match of the season," said Jane. The two girls posed for their selfie and then silenced their phones for the match, and put them back in their tennis bags.

The other players on Jane's team had found their assigned courts as well, and were preparing to play. Jane saw that Brandi was on court six, right next to Jane and Peaches, so she turned to face the other way towards the school. She could see the school bus in the driveway that had transported the opposing team, and the players from the other team were streaming down the paved path to their respective courts.

"Don't look now but there is a guy leaning against the fence over there staring at us," whispered Peaches, as she leaned in toward Jane.

"Where?" said Jane. She started to look around.

"I said don't look," said Peaches. "He's just to the right of the lady in the orange shirt, towards the school building."

Jane cut her eyes around without turning her head. "Does he have sandy hair and a light blue tee shirt with a monster truck on it and jeans?"

"Yes, he's standing by the fence, closest to the

light pole."

Jane turned her head towards the man. He immediately started looking down at his phone. "I have no idea who he is. I've never seen him before. He did seem like he was watching us, though. Maybe he likes our outfits."

"Not likely," chuckled Peaches. "He's giving me the creeps." Peaches took her racquet out of her bag and sat down on the bench. There wasn't a lot of seating for spectators, so people were just milling around as they arrived. The few rows of bleachers filled up fast. There were mostly parents and some of the other students who came to watch.

Jane recognized most of the people, but no one from Jane's family would be there today to watch her play. Her grandparents came to most of her matches, but they were out of town on a cruise for two weeks. They won the cruise and had a limited option of when to take it.

Ever since her mom died when she was six years old, Jane had spent a lot of time with Grandma Helen and Grandpa Dan, whenever her dad went on business trips. Jane's dad, Bill Teaberry, traveled frequently for business for the last few years, so he wasn't around to watch many of Jane's tennis matches.

Today's match was a long one. They needed to win two out of three possible sets to take the match. Jane and Peaches won the first set, 6-3 and lost the second set 5-7. They had to go to a third "decider" set, as each team had won a set. The third set went to 6-6 and they ended up in a nine-point tie-break. The team with the first five points would win the set.

Now Jane really felt the pressure. She hated it when it was down to a tie-break, where one point could determine a win or a loss. She always hoped to win earlier so she wouldn't have to play any tie-breaks. The tie-break went to 5-4, in favor of the opponents. The last ball skimmed the top of the net and dropped over on Jane's side, where there was no way she or Peaches could get to it.

Argh, thought Jane. *What a way to end the season.* Jane and Peaches walked to the net and reached over to congratulate their opponents with a handshake, and then headed to the bench. Luckily, with her dad working in Washington D.C., and her grandparents away on the cruise, no one in the family saw her lose the match.

Jane spotted the man with the monster truck shirt watching them again. They sat on the bench and took their time to grab a drink and towel off. Peaches pulled out her sports drink and started gulping it. "I really need those electrolytes after a long, hot match. I'm super thirsty. And hungry, too." She grabbed a protein bar out of her tennis bag.

"Want half?" she offered, holding it out to Jane.

Jane reached out to accept half of Peaches' protein bar. "Thanks," she said, without taking her eyes off the man. "He's still watching us."

"I see him," replied Peaches, as she was careful not to turn her head towards him. The two girls rested for a few minutes more, while the crowd began to clear. They packed up their tennis bags before walking off the court and went back inside the school.

"I have to stop by my locker," said Peaches, as she headed down the nearly empty hallway. "We did our best, Jane, and we played really well. Don't sweat it. I'll see you tomorrow."

"See you later, Peaches. Your serve was amazing today," said Jane, as she headed in the opposite direction toward the parking lot.

Harry, the team coach, stopped Jane in the hallway. It was obvious that Coach Harry had spent most of his life out in the sun playing tennis, from his sun-drenched skin and sun-bleached hair. Dressed in his black athletic shorts and orange polo shirt with the school logo, and carrying a clipboard, he stood out from the teenagers in the hallway.

"Hey, Jane," he said. "That was a really tough match, and I'm proud of how you two girls played."

"Yeah, thanks. We lost, though," sighed Jane.

"I know," said Coach Harry, in his gravelly voice. "But you put in the time and the effort in practice. Believe me, I've noticed that about you, and Peaches, too. You just need to have more confidence, Jane. You have to expect to win."

"I do expect to win, Harry. That's tougher than it sounds. The other team played great today, better than I've ever seen them play. It doesn't help to have Brandi always putting me down, either. A captain should be trying to lift up her team, not trash people right before a match," Jane replied.

"Well, that's true," said Coach Harry. "And I've talked to her about it. But you can't let other people's words and behavior get to you. I'm not sure what she hopes to accomplish by acting that way, but don't let it crush your confidence. You are a good player, Jane."

"Thanks, Harry. I do appreciate you saying that."

"Confidence comes from within you, not from what others say or think," Harry continued. "You know you are a skilled player and I've seen you improve each year. I thought you did well today on your angles and overheads, and you had some great serves. It's important that you've been diligent about practicing, and it shows in how you play."

"I sure do try," replied Jane. "I just want to be really good at something. I don't care how hard I have to work for it."

"I know," said Harry. "You can be a successful player. I know this was your last high school match, but you still have college to look forward to. I hope you'll stick with it."

Coach Harry and Jane's Grandpa Dan had been great influences on her life. With Jane's dad having to travel so much for his job, she relied on both of them for encouragement. She heard what he said about confidence, but it wasn't easy to become confident, just because he told her to do it.

Harry often told stories about some of the women's teams he coaches. They were all competitive, for sure, whether they were college teams or career leagues. Harry had said he never understood all the issues that seemed to come up, as one of the teams even got into a big dispute about what to have for the team lunch. He always tried to stay out of it, and give good advice, which always landed somewhere around working on your own confidence and skills, and not worrying so much about other people's egos.

Somehow his stories never helped fix Jane's problems, although he tried. Jane loved tennis, but she was kind of happy that high school was almost over, and she wouldn't be joining the local college team if Brandi was on it. She needed a break from being bullied.

Jane's friend, Rachel Appelworth, was waiting outside the door to the parking lot. She had known Rachel since elementary school. However, they had only really become good friends later on in high school. Rachel wasn't on the tennis team, but she understood the mindset for sports, because she played softball.

Rachel was shorter than most of the girls on her softball team, but had an athletic build and could outrun anyone on the team, even the girls with the longest legs. She pitched in most games, and felt pressured to strike out as many players as possible. Rachel felt the team depended on her to keep the batters from getting on base.

Rachel had waited around after school to watch Jane play and then head home with her. "You and Peaches played well today, Jane. You made them earn every point. Nobody hates to lose more than I do, but you must have felt like you had some great shots, didn't you? I saw them!" said Rachel.

"I guess," replied Jane. "You know it never feels

good to lose. It's just as well that Grandma and Grandpa weren't here for this one."

"It wouldn't have mattered if they saw you lose a match. They would have been here if they could have. My parents rarely can come to my softball games," said Rachel, "since they both work full-time. It's nice that your grandparents are retired and can come to most of the matches after school."

"It has been great," agreed Jane. The girls started walking towards Jane's dark blue Jeep Cherokee. It had been her grandpa's old car and he gave it to Jane instead of trading it in on his new one. Jane loved how comfortable it was to drive, and she especially liked having four-wheel drive in the winter months. She knew Grandpa had taken great care of it, so it was in excellent condition. She named it Bernice to make it her own.

"Do you know who that guy is standing by the gate?" asked Rachel, nodding her head to indicate where he was standing. "The tall guy in the tee shirt and jeans. He seems to be waiting for someone. He's looking at his watch now, but he looked like he was watching us a minute ago."

When Jane looked over at him, he suddenly started walking away. "Oh, yeah. Monster truck guy. I saw that same guy earlier, watching Peaches and me before the match," said Jane.

"Well, he was standing there watching us intently and I saw him talking to Brandi Brown a few minutes ago. But, of course, now that we're looking at him, he's walking away. I've never seen him before.

Wonder what he's up to," said Rachel.

"I hope he's nobody I have to worry about," said Jane. "Let's go home," she said, as they packed their bags into Bernice and got in.

Now that she had turned eighteen, Jane was going to be staying by herself for the first time at her grandparents' house, just for two weeks. Well, she wouldn't be completely alone. Rachel was staying with her. They were just a few days away from graduation and had several graduation parties to attend. They had a fun time planned.

Jane had been living with her grandparents in West Midland, Ohio, ever since her father was transferred to northern Virginia, right before her senior year in high school. Jane grew up just a few blocks away from her grandparents before her dad was transferred. She didn't want to move away in her senior year of high school, so her dad let her live with her grandparents full-time, to graduate with her friends. Plus, she wanted to stay in town to attend the local college in the fall.

West Midland is a small village nestled in trees in southwestern Ohio. It has four beautiful parks, a college campus, a hospital, and a beautiful historic library. You could walk to the historic town square from just about anywhere in the village. Most residents who grew up in the village cherished their childhood years attending small town type events with a tight-knit community. Jane loved growing up in West Midland, just like her parents had.

Jane checked her phone messages when she got into the car. There was one from her dad to call him.

She was disappointed that he couldn't come to her match, but she knew he had a lot of responsibility with his job. She didn't completely understand his job, but she knew he was an executive in a large company in Washington, D.C. He commuted from Virginia, since it was more expensive to live in D.C.

"I have a message from my dad to call him," Jane told Rachel. "I better do it now so I don't forget."

"Hi Dad, what's up?"

"Hi Janie." He hesitated. "How was your match?"

"We lost," sighed Jane.

"Aww, I'm sorry, Pumpkin. You'll do better next time, huh?" he said sympathetically.

"This was the last one, Dad, the season is over. No more tennis this year," said Jane. Her voice dropped.

"I know, but you're not finished playing tennis. And every time you play you get a little better. I hope you'll keep playing during the summer," coached Dad. "Rachel and Peaches are still staying with you tonight, right?"

"Peaches has family in town and couldn't come, but yes, Rachel is staying over and is with me now. We are headed home."

"Good. I'll be there as soon as I can for your graduation. Drive carefully," said Dad.

"I will. See you then, Dad," replied Jane as she hung up. Jane knew her dad always worried about her safety, as her mom was killed in a car accident on her way home from work. He never got over the loss of her mom. His constant worries about her safety made Jane fearful sometimes – that was the message that was coming across to her, and she struggled with it. She thought about telling her dad about the guy at the tennis match that was watching them, but wasn't sure at this point whether she was being overly fearful. She didn't want to concern her dad for no reason.

Jane had loved having her grandparents all to herself this past school year and really depended on them. She felt closer to them than ever now that she had been with them every day. Her dad was busy, so living with her retired grandparents had been fun. Grandma Helen was always cheerful, and Grandpa Dan was always willing to listen and give advice.

CHAPTER TWO

HOME LIFE

JANE SMILED WHEN she could see the large spruce trees at each side of her grandparents' driveway. She had always loved coming to visit her grandparents when she was a child, and still felt a bit of excitement as she approached the house.

The front of the house was built with stone, and had a large picture window at the front of the living room. The front yard that seemed gigantic when she was a small child felt as though it shrunk a little each year as she grew up. She was always happy to be here, even though she had been living here all of this year.

She pulled into her grandparents' driveway and drove to the back of the house and parked outside the garage next to the maple tree. The tree was large enough to shade the entire back porch, and had a bench under it where Jane had spent many hours reading or drawing as she grew up. A beautiful garden surrounded the patio, which Jane's grandma lovingly cared for each spring and summer.

The large, open back yard was big enough to play kickball, as she had done many times over the years with the neighbor kids. Jane fondly remembered how her grandpa let her ride along with him on the riding lawn mower when she was younger. Along the edge of the backyard was a row of six fully grown apple trees. She enjoyed helping her grandpa pick apples every summer for as long as she could remember.

"Just a few more days of school and we're done," said Jane, as she and Rachel loaded their school backpacks onto their shoulders and headed to the back door of the house. Jane also carried her tennis bag and a science project, so she was struggling to carry everything to the door.

Rachel was also managing a suitcase, since she would be staying with Jane for two weeks, so she set it down beside the car to help Jane. "Can't wait," said Rachel with a smile.

Just as Jane was about to open the back door, she was startled by someone else approaching behind her. She almost dropped her key.

"Hi there, Jane," said Bob, the next-door neighbor. Bob was in his fifties, and was lean, with thinning brown hair that was sprinkled with gray. He was wearing one of his many Hawaiian shirts today, along with khaki-colored Bermuda shorts, white socks and brown sandals. She turned to see Bob standing in the driveway.

"Oh, hi Bob. You startled me," said Jane, gripping the key in her hand and juggling her tennis bag. She had met Bob last year at a neighborhood picnic, where everyone on the street was invited. It was in the backyard at Dick and Dottie's house. They were the neighbors who lived on the other side of her grandparents' house. Grandma and Grandpa's neighbors were all pretty nice and had frequent picnics and social gatherings. She knew Dick and Dottie better than most of the neighbors, since they lived right next door and were friends of her grandparents.

There was something offensive about Bob that made Jane uncomfortable when he was around. He always seemed sweaty and reeked of cologne. She didn't know him well, although he always seemed to be around. Jane wasn't sure what he did for a living, but she remembered that he worked in some sort of insurance work. She sometimes wondered how he was able to dress in Hawaiian shirts for work, as she often saw him in the afternoons after school when most people were still at work.

She didn't think her grandparents ever seemed happy to see Bob, although they always smiled and were polite to him. You could never tell whether or not her grandparents liked someone or not, because they were nice to everyone. They never invited him over for dinner or any other social activity, but he had been in the house on a few occasions for one reason or another.

"I just want to make sure you know I'm next door here, if you need anything while your grandparents are gone. I can come in and help you with whatever you need now, if you like," Bob suggested.

"Um, thanks Bob, but we're fine. It was nice of you to offer."

"How long will they be gone?" asked Bob.

"I – I'm not sure exactly. Not long," said Jane, as she tried to turn away to head into the house. "Sorry, this stuff is heavy and I have to go."

"Well, uh, okay. See you later." Bob stepped back, and turned to walk across the driveway toward his house. Jane quickly opened the door and she and Rachel slipped inside. Jane felt much better, once she and Rachel were inside the house and the door was locked.

Bob had admired some of the artwork hanging around the house on past visits. He seemed to know something about a couple of the paintings that Jane's grandparents had on the wall. Jane assumed it was because of his insurance work.

"He's so strange," said Jane. "I'm not sure what it is about him, but he makes me uneasy."

"Yeah, I got the same vibe," replied Rachel. "Is the door locked?"

"Yep, it's locked," said Jane. She set down all of her stuff and plopped down on the sofa in the living room. Jane breathed in the sweet smell of vanilla that she associated with her grandparents' house. For the first time today, she felt like she could relax for a minute.

"Oh rats," said Rachel. "I have to go back out and grab my suitcase. I couldn't carry everything in one trip."

As Jane peered through the window to see if Bob was gone, she saw him still standing in the driveway talking on his phone. "I'll stand here by the door," said Jane. Rachel ran out to grab her suitcase, but luckily Bob was still on the phone and didn't say anything to her. She came back in and Jane locked the door behind her, then sat back down in the living room to relax for a minute.

The neat, orderly home was indicative of Jane's grandparents' personalities. Her grandmother loved aqua blue, so the décor of the home had a light airy feel to it. She also loved birds and you could tell by the bird knick-knacks on the shelf, and the needlepointed bird pillows on the chairs. It almost had a tropical feel to it, with the color scheme and some of the paintings on the walls in the living room and the hallway.

Jane loved the seascape painting over the fireplace. It was her favorite. Her grandma called it "Sandpipers by the Sea." It reminded Jane of vacations at the beach with her grandparents and her dad.

It was always quiet and peaceful when she was home with them. She could hear the vintage glass German dome clock on the mantel ticking and whirring as the four-ball pendulum spun around. The house seemed quieter now that Jane was home without her grandparents here.

Jane's grandma often hummed softly as she went about her day. Her grandpa was organized and orderly with his daily projects, and always busy. He had a woodworking shop in the basement where Jane normally would hear sawing and other machinery during the day, but now it lay quiet.

Jane just wanted to feel accepted in her world. She felt like every time she was working hard at something, there was someone out there working against her, and she didn't have a mom to stand up for her. She felt different from the other kids, not having a mom or even a stepmom in her life. Her dad never remarried. He didn't even go out on dates, as far as Jane knew.

Jane realized she was dependent on her grandparents more than other kids would be, as they were the most stable influence on her life that she had since her mom died. Even though they grew up in a different time and couldn't always relate to the issues in Jane's life, she relied on them and wished she could stay with them forever. Jane was glad that Rachel would be staying with her for the two weeks that her grandparents were away. She wasn't ready to handle being home alone.

"I'm gonna put my bags away in my room," said Jane. "I'll be back in a minute."

"Okay," replied Rachel, as she relaxed into a chair by the fireplace. Jane grabbed her bags from the living room and headed down the hallway on the first floor to her bedroom. She dropped her backpack on her bed, and her tennis bag on the floor.

Then she sat down in her mom's old rocker for a few minutes and rocked. This was the same rocker her mom used to sit in to rock her when she was a baby, and it gave her some comfort to have it in her room.

She grabbed her worn out stuffed dog, Ralphie, when she sat down. Ralphie had been given to her by her mom when she was just a toddler, and had served her well over the years to reassure her when she needed it. Jane had several items that had belonged to her mom that she didn't really remember, but felt that having them would somehow keep her mom closer to her.

Suddenly, there was a knock at the front door. "Someone's at the door, Jane," yelled Rachel from the living room. Jane came to the living room and peeked out the window to see who was there. There was a well-dressed woman at the door, carrying a clipboard. She had a hefty amount of makeup and teased blonde hair down to her shoulders, bright pink lipstick, and she was wearing a business suit with a plum-colored jacket and silk blouse. Jane could see a silver Cadillac parked in the driveway with a magnetic real estate sign on the front passenger door.

"Who the heck is that?" said Jane. She felt uncomfortable having to answer the door at all. She wished she could be invisible while her grandparents were gone, and not have to worry about dealing with strangers.

"No idea," said Rachel. "Maybe you don't need to answer the door."

"She doesn't look dangerous or anything," replied Jane. She felt uneasy as she partially opened the door. "Can I help you?"

"Hi there! Are you the owner of the house?" said the woman.

"Um no, can I help you with something?" Jane

replied.

"I'm Angela Mott. I'm with Mott and Swift Real Estate. I was showing a house down the street and my buyers said they really would be interested in this house if it was for sale. So, I thought I'd come check to see if the owners might be interested in considering an offer?"

Angela flashed a big wide smile at Jane, and blinked her big eyes a couple of times. She reminded Jane of an owl on a cartoon show she used to watch. It took Jane a minute to register what Angela had said, since she talked so fast. "I doubt it, but I can give them your card if you want," Jane offered.

"Are they home? asked Angela.

"They're busy," replied Jane. She was starting to feel beads of sweat forming on her forehead.

"Oh, okay. Do you know when they will be free?" Angela persisted.

"Not exactly," said Jane, wishing she could get Angela to leave. She took a step back from the door and started to close it slightly.

"Well, okay. Here is my card. Please ask them not to delay because I don't know how long they might be interested," Angela persevered.

Jane reached out and took the card. "Okay, got it. Thanks." Jane started to close the door again.

"Well, okay, bye," said Angela, looking rather disappointed. She blinked a few more times. Angela went back to her silver Caddy and Bob was still out in the driveway.

Jane saw him talking to Angela for a few minutes

before she left. *What is he doing out there?* Jane thought to herself, as she quickly closed the door and locked it.

"So," said Rachel, "where am I staying?"

"Well," said Jane, "I guess you'll be staying upstairs, so you can have your own room."

"That works," replied Rachel. "Just show me the way."

Jane's grandparents also had a bedroom on the first floor, and there was another room for her grandpa's office. The upstairs was like a Cape Cod style home, with two bedrooms that had slanted ceilings, and a bathroom in between them. Even though the rooms weren't large, it felt spacious since there wasn't a lot of furniture up there. Both rooms were now used as guest rooms. Jane's dad stayed in one of them sometimes when he visited.

"Follow me," said Jane, as she headed up the stairs by the front door. Rachel grabbed her suitcase and backpack and followed Jane up the stairs. Jane pulled a couple of blue towels for Rachel out of the linen closet in the hallway. "Here is the bathroom at the top of the stairs, and then you can stay in this room on the left. It already has clean sheets on the beds," said Jane. "My dad usually stays in the other one when he visits."

The bedroom had plenty of windows and light, with white curtains framing the windows. The bedspreads on the twin beds were blue and white in a swirly pattern, and there was a white dresser with a big mirror. Jane set the towels on a small comfy chair that was in the corner next to a small table with a reading lamp. There were some paintings of bluebirds on the walls. Rachel looked around the room. "What do you think?" asked Jane with a smile.

"It's great," replied Rachel. "Thanks! It's cheerful and peaceful."

"I'll go downstairs and let you get settled," said Jane. She went back to the living room and sat down on the aqua blue sofa under the window across from the fireplace. Jane suddenly felt quite different and a little uncomfortable knowing her grandparents wouldn't be home soon. She hoped they were having fun on the cruise. She thought they deserved to have a good time.

Rachel came downstairs in a few minutes and plopped down on the sofa with Jane. "So where did your grandparents go on this cruise?"

Jane said, "They left from Florida yesterday and they are supposed to visit some of the Caribbean islands. It should be a lot of fun for them, since they are retired and don't need to worry about work piling up or anything."

"That's great," said Rachel. "It must have been expensive for two weeks."

"Actually, no," said Jane. "They won the trip. They didn't have much of a choice of when to take it, so they're gonna miss my graduation. I know they feel just awful about that. But we'll have photos, and I didn't want them to give it up just for that, you know? I don't remember them saying they entered any contests, though."

"Yeah, I wouldn't want to give up a two-week

vacation just to watch someone graduate from high school, either," Rachel laughed.

"I know they felt bad about not being here for it, but I told them not to." Jane shrugged her shoulders. "I always assumed they would be around for my graduation, because they come to everything else that I do, but that's just how it turned out. I'm excited that my cousin, Ashley, will be back in town, so she will be here, and my dad is coming. He travels a lot, so I'm lucky that he'll at least be able to make it to the ceremony."

CHAPTER THREE

GRADUATION AT LAST

THREE DAYS LATER, Jane and Rachel dressed for graduation. Their caps and gowns were white, so they both had bought new white dresses to wear underneath, as instructed by the school's graduation rule sheet. Jane had selected a cute dress that she thought she would be able to wear on other occasions, so she was happy for an excuse to buy the new dress.

The girls hopped into Bernice, Jane's blue Jeep Cherokee, and headed to the Civic Center where it was being held. There wasn't a big enough venue in West Midland to hold events like graduations, but they didn't have to drive far outside of the village to get to the Civic Center.

"When is your dad coming?" asked Rachel, as they cruised down the highway. Jane was checking her rear view mirror periodically for a black pickup truck that continued to stay behind them. She changed lanes to go around a Volkswagen Bug, and then traversed back to the right lane. The truck passed the Bug, too, and stayed right with Bernice.

"Um," said Jane, as she turned her focus back on the conversation. "His flight gets in right before the ceremony, so he'll be coming straight there from the airport," she replied, as she turned off the exit to the East Fork Civic Center.

Jane pulled into the parking lot and started looking for a place to park. The pickup truck followed them into the lot, but then slowed down and turned down a different row of cars heading away from them.

"I didn't realize there would be so many people here," said Rachel, looking out the window. She noticed a rather large crowd of people heading towards the door of the building.

"Yeah, wow," said Jane. "This place is huge. Let me know if you see a good spot."

"There's one," Rachel pointed to the spot. "Beside the red sedan." Jane parked Bernice and she and Rachel grabbed their graduation caps and gowns out of the back and followed the crowd inside. There were greeters inside the main door to help them figure out where to go.

"Boy this place is crowded," said Jane as she struggled to get around the people in the large hallway, trying not to lose track of Rachel. "Let me know if you spot my dad out in the audience," Jane requested. "Although it won't be easy with all these people."

"I will," promised Rachel, as they followed the signs for graduates and took their places in alphabetical order. After the ceremony, Jane went out to the hallway, where there was a table set up with light refreshments. She spotted Peaches and her family getting refreshments.

"Hi there, Jane," said Peaches' mom, as she gave her a hug. "Are your grandparents here?"

"No, I'm afraid not, Dr. Parker," said Jane. "They aren't back yet. But my dad is here somewhere, and so is my cousin."

"Oh, good," said Peaches' mom. "I haven't seen them yet."

Peaches' mom was a doctor at the West Midland Hospital, and her dad taught archaeology at the local college. Jane had enjoyed hearing his dig stories on several occasions at dinner. Peaches often worried that her mom might pressure her to go to medical school, as she had not yet decided what she wanted to do after high school. Peaches and Jane took some photos together in their caps and gowns with the assistance of Peaches' dad.

Jane spotted her six-foot tall cousin, Ashley Fink, who is four years older than Jane. Jane was pleased that she came to see her graduate. Ashley had just graduated from college and had recently come home to West Midland to begin searching for a job. "Ah, there is my cousin," said Jane. "Hopefully I can catch her before she disappears in the crowd. I'll see you later." Jane walked quickly down the hallway to where Ashley was standing.

"Hey, Jane," said Ashley. "Congrats!!! You made it through high school!" Ashley gave Jane a big bear hug, lifting her up off the ground. Jane chuckled to herself to see Ashley dressed in her usual basketball shorts and high-top gym shoes. She wasn't keen on dressing up when it wasn't an actual requirement.

"Thanks, Ash! And thanks for coming." Jane grinned from ear to ear. She was pleased to see her cousin back in town. She had missed her when she was gone.

"Of course, I want to see my little cousin graduate."

"I see you dressed up for the occasion," Jane smiled and chuckled.

"Of course, I did." Ashley smiled back and winked at Jane. She held out one foot.

"These shoes are new! Do you like them?"

Jane looked down at the high-tops. "They're great," replied Jane. "I love them."

Jane spotted Brandi Brown coming down the hallway and turned to look the other way, but Brandi spotted her and started heading towards her. Jane took a step behind Ashley to avoid her. Brandi's two besties, Heather and Brittany were with her, as usual. She wondered if Brandi felt more powerful having them by her side, like two guard dogs.

"Don't move," Jane said to Ashley. "That's Brandi Brown over there with the blonde hair and those two other girls. Let me stay here behind you until she goes on her way."

"Um, okay," said Ashley, looking puzzled. "Okay, they stopped and now she's talking to some guy."

"Good, thanks," said Jane.

"You look kind of shaken up. Are you afraid of her?" asked Ashley.

"I don't know. I just prefer to avoid her. That's all," replied Jane.

"Don't let that girl push you around," said Ashley.

"I know... I know," replied Jane, looking down at the floor.

"Your dad is here somewhere. I sat with him, but we got separated when he went to the restroom. I'm not sure you'll be able to find him in this crowd," Ashley explained.

"We need to get back to the refreshment table to meet Rachel," said Jane. "C'mon."

"Okey dokey," said Ashley, following her to the table. Rachel was already there waiting.

Jane felt her cell phone buzz in her pocket. "Oh, here is a message from Dad. It looks like he just left the Civic Center and will stop by the house after graduation. Rats. I guess there's no point in sticking around then. Ready to go?"

"Sure," said Rachel. "I already saw my parents. I'm ready to go."

"I have no other reason to stay," agreed Ashley. "Let's bolt."

"Do you want to come home with us and hang out for a while?" asked Jane.

"Can't today," replied Ashley. "I have a job interview this afternoon."

"Some other time then. Soon I hope," said Jane.

Jane, Ashley, and Rachel went out to the parking lot and Jane saw the same guy that was lurking around at the tennis match. He was standing by the fence looking at his phone. *I wonder what "Monster Truck" is doing here*, wondered Jane. *Maybe he is Brandi's brother or something*, she thought. *He must be related to someone on the tennis team, since he was there for the match.* She couldn't remember if Brandi had an older brother. She did remember that Brandi said she'd be sorry if she lost the last match, but hopefully she was just being mean and wasn't referring to anything specific. But just in case, she planned to avoid anyone that had any connection to her.

Ashley headed for her orange Jeep Wrangler. It had big tires and a power winch on the front bumper, with little rubber ducks lining the dashboard. The top was down and all of the doors were removed. "I'm parked over this way," she said, as she indicated the direction of her car.

Jane looked over at Ashley's Jeep. "There's no mud on your car," she observed.

Ashley laughed. "I just got home yesterday. I haven't been off-roading yet. I will soon, I hope. See ya later," she said, as she hopped into the driver's seat.

"Good luck on your interview," said Jane, hoping Ashley would change into something more appropriate for a job interview.

"Thanks," replied Ashley. As Ashley pulled out of the parking lot, Jane realized she never asked what kind of job she was trying to get. Jane and Rachel put their caps and gowns in the back of Bernice, and headed back to the house. Jane maneuvered Bernice down the long driveway to the back of her grandparent's house, hoping Bob wasn't going to show up again. Her dad was already parked there.

"No Bob today." Jane smiled triumphantly, as she parked the car.

"Good," said Rachel. The girls went inside the house through back door.

"Janie!" said her dad with a big smile and arms out wide. "I'm so sorry I couldn't find you after the graduation, but I did get to see you walk across the stage. Congratulations, Pumpkin. I'm proud of you."

"Thanks Dad," beamed Jane, as her dad gave her a big hug. "I can't believe that high school is over," she said with a relaxed smile crossing her face. She suddenly felt a little taller.

"I can't stay long," said her dad, "as I have a big meeting in the morning. I really wish I didn't have to go."

"Don't worry, I understand," sighed Jane. She didn't want him to leave so soon, but smiled as she said it so he wouldn't feel bad about it.

Jane's dad still struggled with the loss of Jane's mother. Her mom, Jane and her brother, Michael, had been his whole world. It was so sudden when she was in the accident. He couldn't have even imagined how quickly she was pulled away from them. She was so young and full of life. He felt lucky that he had his parents' support and help raising Jane and Michael, but he still felt lost sometimes. With all the travel he did for work lately, he didn't have a lot of time to have close friends or meet anyone new.

With Michael living overseas for the last few years, he focused on keeping Jane safe and happy and doing what he could so she would grow up to be successful. He felt too distant sometimes and wasn't sure how to close the gap. Conversations with Jane ended up being awkward sometimes, because he didn't know quite what to say.

He tried hard to let Jane have enough freedom but he worried about her constantly. He realized he probably should hold back more with his worries. He just couldn't stand it if something happened to her, as well. Emotionally, he still found it difficult to talk about Jane's mother, and hoped one day he would be able to share more about her with Jane. He choked up every time he tried to talk about her.

Jane, Rachel and Jane's dad sat down in the living room. "This was a big day for you girls," said Jane's dad. "How do you feel about it?"

"I have mixed feelings, I guess," said Jane.

"I feel a little sad, I think," said Rachel. "High school is what I know, and now it's over."

"I understand that," said Jane's dad. "But new and exciting experiences will replace that. You probably felt the same way when you went from middle school to high school. Everything changes but you will adapt to the next part of your life, just as you always have."

Jane's dad pulled out a card with a check in it and handed it to Jane. "Here's a little money for something special," he said.

Jane opened the card and read it silently and smiled. "Thanks, Dad. I love you."

"I love you too, Pumpkin," he replied. "I'm proud of you."

"Thanks, Dad," said Jane.

"Oh, and I have one more thing for you." He pulled a little box out of his pocket. Jane smiled when she saw the box, wondering what it could be.

"Thank you," she said, looking surprised. She started unwrapping the box.

"It was your mother's," said her dad. "I found it when I was unpacking at the new house. She used to wear it all the time and I know she would want you to have it. Consider it a gift from her. "

Jane beamed. *What could be more special than a gift from my mom?* she thought. She opened the box to find a gold chain with what looked like a coin hanging from it.

"Wow, this is interesting," said Jane. "Is this a real coin? There's something engraved on the back in another language."

"Yes… I'm not sure and I don't know what it means," said her dad. "We'll figure it out. But for now, congratulations also from your mom."

Jane gave her dad a hug. "Thanks Dad. This means a lot to me."

"I know," he said.

Jane immediately put the necklace on. "I'm never taking this off," she said.

"I'm really sorry I can't stay longer, but I need to get back to work."

"I'm really glad you could come, even for a little while. Especially since Grandma and Grandpa couldn't be here," said Jane.

"Me, too," said Jane's dad. After sharing a snack with the girls, Jane's dad left.

CHAPTER FOUR

A NIGHTTIME SURPRISE

IN THE MIDDLE of the night, Jane heard a loud clunk in the living room. Then it sounded like the front door closed. She froze in her bed under the covers, listening intently. Jane was afraid to breathe, in case someone could hear her. Everything was quiet now, except for the sound of Jane's heart beating loudly. Eyes wide open, there was no way she could sleep until she checked it out. She waited for what seemed like the longest time, but there was no more noise.

After about twenty minutes of hiding under the covers, Jane got up and donned her white terry cloth bathrobe. With the lights still off and utilizing the flashlight on her cell phone, Jane crept down the hallway to the living room. She shined the flashlight around the room and didn't see anything moving. She held her breath and flipped on the light switch.

Jane couldn't believe her eyes. There was a man lying on the living room floor in front of the fireplace. He was face down with a small knife in his hand. Jane gasped silently and put her hand over her mouth. She held her breath while she ran on tiptoes back to her room and shut the bedroom door and locked it. She called 911.

"Please, please send the police! 7200 Maple Lane. There's a man in the house and he looks d-dead. Please h-h-hurry!" she pleaded. After hanging up the phone, Jane sat down in her rocker and pulled her knees up to her chin. Tears began to stream down her face and she started trembling. She grabbed Ralphie and hugged him tightly. She rocked back and forth, trying to calm herself down.

Jane took a deep breath and called her cousin, Ashley. "Hi Ash, sorry to wake you," Jane whispered. "Can you come over and bring Edward with you? I'll explain when you get here."

"Uh, okay," said Ashley, rubbing her eyes and looking at the clock. "Why are you whispering? Wait… what the heck … it's three A.M. What's wrong? Never mind. I'll be right there. I'll leave a note for my parents so I don't have to wake them."

"Thanks Ash," sniffled Jane. She hung up the phone and started rocking again.

Ashley was someone that Jane could count on, no questions asked, but Jane was usually reluctant to ask for support. Jane had missed having Ashley around for the four years she was away at college, and she was really glad to have her back in town for good. Since

Ashley had just finished college and didn't have a job yet, she was living back home nearby with her parents. She was happy to be back home in West Midland and her regular gym workout routine.

Jane stayed locked in her room until she saw flashing lights out the window in the driveway and there was a loud banging on the door. "West Midland police! Open the door!" they yelled. Jane jumped up immediately and tied her robe. She scurried through the living room on tiptoes and opened the door.

Jane was relieved when the police came inside the house and took over. "Over there by the fireplace," she directed them, barely looking over in that direction. Two of the officers checked the downstairs of the house before attending to the body on the floor. Jane stood back slightly behind one of the officers near the door, now just beginning to let herself take in the scene.

Wait - is that a Hawaiian shirt? she wondered to herself, just now noticing the details of the man on the floor. She stared at the shirt for a moment before she noticed the khaki shorts and sandals.

"He's dead," said one officer, who was kneeling over the victim. He verified by checking his pulse. "Help me turn this guy over."

The two officers turned the body over. For the first time, Jane could see his face and she recognized the victim. "That's Bob from next door!" she exclaimed. "Why would he be here?"

"I don't know, Miss. What's his last name?" said Officer Kemp.

"Sheppard. Bob Sheppard. That's about all I know about him. He lives next door."

"I don't see any blood on him, except on the blade of the knife in his hand," said Officer Smith, kneeling beside the body. "He has marks around his neck indicating strangulation. It looks like there was a struggle here. Can I assume these items were not knocked over like this when you went to bed?"

Jane looked around the room at the mess. A lamp was knocked over, and some books and knick-knacks from the bookshelf were on the floor. One of the fireplace chairs was pushed back out of place. The "Sandpipers by the Sea" painting over the fireplace was crooked, and the candlesticks from the fireplace mantel were on the floor. Jane was relieved to see that the dome clock was still safely in place on the end of the mantel.

"You assume correctly," said Jane, bewildered by the scene. She rubbed her hands up and down her arms as she started to shiver nervously, even though it wasn't cold out.

Jane walked down the hallway and into the dining room to look around. She noticed that two of the paintings from the dining room wall were gone. She walked back in the living room where the officers were still working on the scene. "There are two paintings missing from the dining room wall," said Jane.

"I found a couple of paintings leaning against the wall beside the back door," replied Officer Kemp.

"Oh, I didn't see them." Jane walked through the kitchen to the back door to check the two paintings.

"Don't touch anything. You really need to stay out of the way while we assess the scene," said Officer Kemp.

"Okay," called Jane from the kitchen. "I promise I won't touch anything." She came back into the living room. "Yep, those are the ones from the dining room," she reported.

"Please show me your hands," said Officer Smith, as he stood back up from the body.

"What? Why?" said Jane, as she held them out for him to see. Her hands were still trembling. He looked at her face and arms as well, but didn't explain.

"Were you here when the incident occurred?" he asked Jane. "What were you doing?"

"I was asleep in bed!" replied Jane. "I heard a loud clunk and I think I heard the door close."

"Who else lives here?" the officer asked.

Jane replied, "Right now, there is no one living here but me, but my friend Rachel is staying here for two weeks with me.

"Check the upstairs," he said to one of the other officers.

"I don't understand how this happened. How did he get in here?" Jane asked.

"It appears that the back door is unlocked," observed Officer Kemp. "There are no other signs of an attempted entry, so I think we can assume that the door was his avenue into the house."

"I know it was locked when I went to bed," said Jane. "I double-checked it."

"Please review the events of this evening for me."

Officer Smith pulled out his notepad and pen.

Jane took a deep breath and began to recount the events of the evening. "Let's see. My friend Rachel and I had both gone to bed. She is in the upstairs bedroom, and I was in my bedroom downstairs. I was asleep and then I heard a noise. It sounded like a clunk, and then I think I heard a door close. I waited, and then didn't hear anything else for a long time. Then I got up and looked around with my flashlight and found this guy in the living room. That's really all I know."

"And you didn't find him in here and struggle with him?" asked Officer Smith.

"No," said Jane. "I told you, when I came out here and turned on the light, he was lying face down on the floor. No one else was in the room."

"You're sure that's exactly how it happened?" asked Officer Smith.

"Yes, I'm absolutely sure," said Jane.

"What about your friend, where is she?" he asked. Just then, Rachel came downstairs and appeared from the front hallway rubbing her eyes, with one of the officers following behind her. "What's going on?" she asked, squinting at the bright light in the living room.

Jane said, "Oh, Rachel, someone broke in. I heard a noise and found this guy in the living room."

"What about you, Miss?" Officer Smith said to Rachel. "What do you know about the events of this evening?"

"I just now woke up and heard a bunch of commotion. Then this officer came to my door and ordered me downstairs," replied Rachel, looking surprised to see the other officers in the living room. She started to look around and saw the body on the floor. Rachel gasped and put her hand over her mouth.

"Is that the weird guy from next door?" she asked.

"Let me see your hands," requested Officer Smith. Rachel showed him her hands. He inspected her for any visible marks on her arms and face, as well.

"What in the world is going on?" she asked.

"Miss, we have a homicide here. And the two of you seem to be the only ones here."

"What are you trying to say?" asked Jane.

"I'm not saying anything except for the facts," replied the officer.

"Well, I hope you don't think we had anything to do with this," defended Jane. "I don't know what Bob was doing in the house, or what happened to him. He lives next door and was not invited in."

"You obviously knew something happened here, maybe because you were involved," said the officer.

"I wasn't!" said Jane, holding back tears. "I don't know anything about what happened. I was asleep!"

"Miss, I assure you we will get to the bottom of this," said the officer.

Rachel went upstairs to get her cell phone to call her parents. Her chin was trembling and she struggled to get the words out. Tears filled her eyes as she tried to explain to her parents what was happening. She came back to the living room to join Jane. "My parents are on the way over. Sorry, Jane, I want to go home. Please come with me."

"Miss, we'll need your name and contact information before you leave. We'll have more questions for you tomorrow," said Officer Smith. He turned to the other officer and said, "Let's get forensics in here."

Kemp radioed in the request. "Miss, please stay out of the way and don't touch anything until we are finished assessing the scene," he said to Jane.

"Okay," said Jane, still shivering and rubbing her arms. She sat down on the sofa by the window with Rachel to wait for them to finish investigating the scene. Jane grabbed the throw from the back of the sofa, and wrapped herself in it.

While waiting for the forensics team, Officer Smith sat down beside Jane. "How did you know the victim?" he asked.

"Just because he lives next door. This is my grandparents' house and I've been staying with them for the past year."

"Where are they now?"

"They're on a cruise. They've been gone for a few days."

"Oh," said the officer. "How well did they know this guy?"

"I don't know for sure. I don't think they are friends, but he always seems to be around. He stopped me the other day and was asking if I needed anything while my grandparents are gone, so I guess they must have told him about the cruise. He's lived next door for a while. I don't know why in the world he would break into the house in the middle of the night."

"It looks like he was here to steal some paintings, although I'm not sure what he was doing with the knife," said the officer. "I'll need contact information for your grandparents."

"Sure, no problem," said Jane, as she wrote down her grandpa's phone number on the officer's notepad. "But they said they would be out of range on the cruise."

Jane stayed on the sofa watching what was going on and because she felt safer in the room with the officers. Rachel went back upstairs. Just then Dick and Dottie from next door burst through the front door, startling Jane. "What's going on?" shrieked Dottie with a worried look. "Why are the police here?"

Dottie was wearing a silk robe with giant pink flowers and had her hair up in a pink bandana. She had cold cream covering most of her face. She obviously wasn't planning on going out anywhere at this time of night. "We told your grandfather we would keep an eye out for you while they were gone, but we certainly didn't expect anything to happen," said Dick. Dick was dressed in his pajamas, robe, and slides, and had a cigarette in his hand. Jane was used to seeing him only in golf attire or swim trunks, so this was a new look.

"Well, I guess something did happen," said Jane. "I heard some noise in the living room and found Bob in front of the fireplace. I don't know why or what happened, but they said he's dead."

"Oh, my Lord," said Dottie. "That's just terrible!

Poor Bob. What would he be doing in here in the middle of the night?" she said with a puzzled look on her face.

"I have no idea, but the police are working on it," said Jane quietly. She was starting to calm down a bit, and realized she how tired she was. She yawned and shivered a bit, then rewrapped the throw around her. "Thanks for checking, Dottie, but I don't think there's anything you can do right now."

"Well, you let us know if you need anything at all, dear," said Dottie, as she patted Jane on the shoulder. "We'll be right next door."

"I will," said Jane. She looked up at Dottie, who turned to Dick and whispered something Jane could not hear.

Dick and Dottie went home, after offering their contact information to the police.

Rachel came down the stairs with her suitcase. "My parents are on their way. Please come stay at our house tonight. You shouldn't be here alone and I am scared. I don't want to stay here right now."

Even though Jane understood, she felt a little rejected that Rachel was so quick to leave. She also was upset at what had happened, but felt as though Rachel was running out on her. "I'm not sure what to do," said Jane. "I called my cousin and she is on the way to help me figure it out."

The front door opened again and in walked Rachel's parents. "What in the world is going on?" bellowed Rachel's dad, as one of the police officers held the door open to let them in.

"Sir, please stay over on this side of the room," directed one of the officers.

Rachel's parents headed over to where Rachel was sitting on the sofa beside her suitcase. "What's going on?" her father repeated.

"This guy… I'm not sure, but Jane woke up and found this guy dead in the living room. He's from next door but we don't know how he got in or why he is here," explained Rachel. "Can we go home now?"

"We can't just leave Jane here alone," said Rachel's father. "Jane, are you coming with us? You can't stay here alone."

"My cousin is on her way," said Jane. "I need to talk to her first and figure out what to do next."

Rachel's father looked over at the dead body in front of the fireplace. He sat down and put his head in his hand. "This is just unbelievable and upsetting. It's the last thing I would have expected to happen. Have you called your grandparents?"

"No," said Jane. "They are out of range on the cruise ship. I can't get in touch with them, but I will let my dad know." Just then Ashley arrived through the front door with her black Labrador Retriever, Edward.

Jane's older cousin was mostly muscle, since she lifted weights at the gym on a regular basis. Her hair was pulled back into a long braid, and she wore a bandana that looked like the American flag, a muscle tank top, basketball shorts, and high-top sneakers. Ashley had been intense about her body-building and exercise routine since her early teens, and had become quite strong and a daunting figure with her six-foot frame. Jane admired her greatly, as she was four years older and wasn't afraid of much. She suddenly felt a little safer with Ashley and Edward in the house.

Ashley looked around in surprise at all the police and the dead body, and said, "Wowza! What happened here?"

CHAPTER FIVE

SECRETS REVEALED

Edward dashed straight to Jane when he walked in the door, and showered her with affection. His big wet tongue licked her hands, as she tried to pull them away to pat him on the head. Jane squatted down and gave him a big hug and squeezed him affectionately around the ears. Edward reached for her face with his big tongue, now that it was close enough.

"Stop licking me!" Jane laughed, though she was still trembling from nervousness. "I'm happy to see you too!" Jane was relieved to see both Ashley and Edward.

Edward was a three-year old rescue and was Ashley's constant companion. He was a great dog, and fairly well-trained and overly affectionate. He had been found wandering the streets and no one knew anything about his background. He had no chip to identify him, so there was no way to find anything out about him. He was a bit nervous and uncomfortable the first few days, but he and Ashley meshed like bread and butter, and they were the best of friends. Jane couldn't understand why someone would let such a great dog get lost.

"We really encourage you to come to our house," said Rachel's dad to Jane, with a worried look on his face. "I know your grandparents wouldn't want you to stay here after what happened. We can't just leave you here by yourself."

"I appreciate it," said Jane, as she stood back up from Edward. "I need to talk to Ashley first before I go."

"Wait – what the heck happened here and why are you leaving?" asked Ashley. "Edward and I can stay here with you. We'll be fine. He's a great watchdog."

Jane explained to Ashley what had happened. "I'm not sure what to do now," Jane added.

"You shouldn't leave the house empty, and we'll be okay here together with Edward. Plus, we can ask the police to patrol and keep an eye out."

"Are you sure?" said Jane.

"Of course," said Ashley. "The guy is already dead. I can stay until your grandparents get back."

"Well, okay then," said Jane. "I guess I'll be okay now that Ashley and Edward are here," she told Rachel's father.

"But who killed this Bob guy?" asked Rachel's dad. "Was someone else here too?"

"I don't know," said Jane. "There's no one else

here now. I have no idea what happened, but the police have checked the house."

"Edward is a great watchdog," said Ashley. "We'll be okay here," Ashley assured Rachel's dad. He didn't look convinced. Worry lines still stood out on his forehead.

Jane looked at Rachel's mom who hadn't said a word. Her eyes were wide and her face looked ashen. She clung tightly to Rachel. She seemed as though she was frozen where she was standing. Sometimes Jane was a little jealous of Rachel's closeness with her mom. Rachel had always been a free spirit, and didn't worry about what other people thought. Jane wished she could be a little more of a free spirit, too.

When Jane thought about her own mother, it made her mad sometimes that she couldn't remember much about her. She did remember that when she was younger they had a garden, and Jane remembered picking vegetables with her mother. She sat at the kitchen table and tried to help her mom make bread-and-butter pickles from her great grandmother's recipe. Jane wondered what her mom would do if she were here now.

Her friends' moms, like Rachel's mom, always tried to look out for her, and she always appreciated it, but she always had that empty void, which was especially hard when she tried to remember things about her mom. Jane kept a picture of her on her dresser. Sometimes she would just stare at it, hoping to connect with her mom's spirit. But as the years went on, she felt like the mom in the picture was further and further away from her memory. She missed her every day.

"Make sure to lock all of the doors and windows," said Officer Kemp.

Jane refocused her thoughts back on the reality of the present situation.

"Keep in mind that we still don't know what happened here. You still could be in some danger," said Rachel's dad. "You can come to our house at any time and stay as long as you like," he added.

Jane looked at Ashley and Edward. Ashley nodded her head and winked at Jane. "We've got this."

"Thank you, Mr. Appelworth," said Jane. "I may have to do that, but for tonight, Ashley can help me sort things out here."

"Okay, then," said Rachel's dad reluctantly.

"I'm really sorry to run out on you Jane," said Rachel. "But I don't want to stay. I wish you were coming with me. I'll see you at Jenny's party?"

"Sure," said Jane. "I'll see you there." Rachel gathered her suitcase and backpack, and she and her parents headed out the front door and left. The police continued with their forensics work for a while, and the coroner removed Bob's body.

"We may be back to ask more questions later," said Officer Smith. "We've verified that the house is clear of any other intruders. Keep your doors locked." The police gathered up all their equipment and left.

Suddenly the house was quiet again. Jane's grandparents' peaceful living room now felt strange. She wished her grandparents were home. "I guess I should call my dad?" Jane reluctantly asked Ashley. "He's gonna freak."

Jane picked up her cell phone and called her dad. "He's not answering," she said. "Hi Dad, I realize it's late. I'll call you tomorrow," she said to his voice mail.

"It'll have to wait until morning," Ashley said. "It's the middle of the night and heck, I don't know what good it will do anyway except to worry him. We're fine here with Edward. Aren't we boy, aren't we boy?" she said to the dog. Edward wagged his tail hard and licked Ashley's hand and rubbed his nose on her.

"Yeah, okay," said Jane. "I'm not looking forward to telling him about this, and Grandpa said they wouldn't have cell reception on the cruise. I don't know what to think. Someone else was here. But who? Did Bob have a partner and they got into a fight, or did someone else follow him in that was after him? The whole scenario doesn't make sense."

"And what about the two paintings by the door? It looks like he was stealing them, which when I think about it, makes sense. He showed a lot of interest in the paintings in the living room and hallway, too. How bold of him to sneak in here in the middle of the night, knowing we were here. That really makes me mad," said Jane.

Jane sat down in the chair beside the fireplace, and Ashley sat in the matching chair on the opposite side. "He looked like a weasel to me," said Ashley. "I never met him, but he looked like someone I wouldn't want to know."

"I know what you're saying, but dead people don't

always look their best," said Jane with a smirk. "He always gave me the creeps, though, when he was alive." They sat for a few minutes in silence. Jane was thinking about everything that had just happened.

"Look at this mess," said Jane. "There must have been a doozy of a fight here. The painting over the fireplace is crooked. Maybe that's what he was taking when the fight started. He had a knife in his hand, so there must have been another person here, unless he was trying to cut a painting out of the frame or something."

Jane stood up and straightened the painting and set the candlesticks back on the mantel. Then she picked up some books off the floor that had fallen off the shelf and put them back on the built-in bookcase on the right side of the fireplace. The bookcase moved slightly when she set the books down.

"Something about this bookcase isn't quite right," said Jane. She frowned as she tried to figure out what was wrong. "Ashley look, the bookcase is pulled away from the wall." Jane pulled on it and it opened. "I didn't know this opened!" She suddenly felt stale cool air coming from behind the opening.

"Yikes," said Jane as she stepped back. "What is this?"

"Let me see," said Ashley, as she jumped up and rushed over to the opening. Jane stepped back out of the way to let Ashley take the lead. Ashley pulled out her cell phone and turned on the flashlight and shined it into the opening.

"It's a whole room," said Ashley, her voice

echoing. She shined the flashlight around on the walls until she found a light switch. Ashley flipped the switch to turn on the light.

Jane crept into the room, hiding behind Ashley. "I can't believe it! I never knew this was here." The room was dusty and full of cobwebs. There were empty shelves lining all the walls. The shelves had tags on the edges with numbers and letters on them. There was a single painting on one of the shelves, but the rest of them were empty.

"Looks like a nice painting. I wonder why they keep it in here," Ashley observed.

"I have no idea," said Jane. "Why would they hide a painting in here when they have so many cool ones hanging on the walls? Do you think they forgot about it?"

"It looks like this is all there is. Let's go to bed. We can figure it out in the morning. I'm tired," said Ashley. She yawned.

"I hope I can sleep now. What a night!" Jane was wide-eyed with all that had happened.

CHAPTER SIX

A CLOSER LOOK

THE NEXT MORNING, Jane woke up to hear Edward barking. She was comforted that he was in the house, but apprehensive about why he might be barking. Everything that happened seemed surreal, like a bad dream. She reflected about the events that occurred during the night, and hoped Ashley would investigate the barking and she wouldn't have to do it.

Jane sat up and looked around the room. Suddenly, Edward came bolting into the bedroom with Ashley following.

"Good morning!" Jane said to Edward as he jumped up on the bed to lick Jane's face. Jane scrunched his ears and gave him a hug. He bounced around on the bed for a minute and then settled down beside Jane.

"What's going on with the barking? Should I worry?"

"Oh, no," said Ashley. "He was just barking at the garbage collectors. Everything seems quiet this morning. I took Edward outside for a few minutes and looked around the house, too."

Ashley plopped down on the bed beside Jane and Edward. "Ugh, why are you all sweaty?" asked Jane, pulling the covers up over her face.

"From my morning run," said Ashley. "Five miles this morning. If Edward and I are gonna stay here with you, you're gonna have to start running with me. He likes to run with me, but I left him here with you for protection this morning."

"Well, I do appreciate that," said Jane. "Thank you, Edward. As for me running, I don't know that I could run ten feet."

"You will be soon," promised Ashley. "I'll get you out there. You'll love it!"

Jane just smiled and chuckled. She didn't know what to think about that.

"I was thinking we need to know more about this Bob guy," Ashley continued. "I don't know how deeply the police are gonna investigate, and we need to know who else was in the house last night."

"Do you mean an Internet search?"

"Yes, that too," said Ashley. "But since he lives… lived… right next door, let's go over to his house and look around."

"You mean break in?"

"I wouldn't put it that way. Just kind of look around." Ashley winked at Jane.

"That makes me nervous, but I guess we could

look in the windows and see if we see anything suspicious."

"It'll be fine," assured Ashley. "We have to look out for ourselves and knowledge is everything. We need to know as much about him as we can find out. "

"First, I need to call my dad again," said Jane.

"I guess you'd better." Ashley shrugged her shoulders in agreement.

Just then Jane's cell phone buzzed. She picked it up from the table beside her bed.

"Hi Dad," she said.

"Hi Pumpkin," he replied. "I'm sorry I missed your call. Is everything okay?" he asked.

"Funny you should say that," said Jane. "First, don't worry. I just wanted to let you know about something that happened last night. You know that guy Bob that lives next door?"

"Yes, what do you mean don't worry?"

Jane continued. "Well, he broke in here and it looks like he was trying to steal Grandma's paintings from the dining room. But something happened to him and I found him in the living room dead last night."

"You're sure he's dead?" asked her dad.

"Yes. I don't know what happened, but the police were here and they are investigating, and I'm keeping all the doors locked. Also, Rachel went home, but Ashley and Edward are staying here to protect me."

"So, you don't know anything about what happened?"

"No," Jane replied. "I was asleep. I called the police and they came and handled everything. They said they would investigate and find out what happened."

"Jane, why don't you come stay in Virginia? I'm on the road at the moment, though. You'd be by yourself there, but will probably be safer. Maybe Ashley and Edward could come with you. School is out and you don't really have to be there right now."

"But they're already here, and my friends are here. The police promised to patrol and keep an eye on the house, too. I have a couple of graduation parties that I'd still like to attend. I don't see that I would be safer there with them than here."

Her dad sighed. "I suppose you're right," he said. "You be careful, and check in with me so I know you are alright. Make sure your doors are locked and don't go anywhere alone. Got it?"

"Yes, dad, I promise," said Jane. "Also, Grandpa asked Dottie and Dick to keep an eye out on the house, so they'll be watching, too."

"Okay," said her dad. "I love you, Janie. I wish there was a better solution."

"I love you, too, Dad. I promise I'll be careful. Bye."

Ashley jumped up from her chair the second that Jane hung up the phone, and headed toward the back door. "Now that you have that out of the way, let's go explore!"

Jane could feel the butterflies in her stomach wake up and start dancing vigorously in a circle, and beads of sweat were starting to appear on her forehead. Her palms felt sweaty, too. She hesitated for a moment and took a deep breath. "But I'm still in my pajamas," Jane protested.

"Who cares?" said Ashley. "No one will see you."

Jane sighed. "I hope not." She wanted to know why Bob was in the house, and who killed him, but she wished she didn't have to investigate it herself. She hoped the police would handle it all, but they didn't tell her much about what they would do. They acted like she had something to do with it, and that worried her. If they arrested her, she wouldn't have an opportunity to discover who really did it.

She couldn't let Ashley go alone. She paused for a minute to think. "Okay, let's do it." Jane swallowed hard, and followed Ashley toward the door. "What about Edward? Are we taking him with us?" she asked.

"No, he can stay here and wait for us. Bob's dead, so I don't think we'll need any protection." Ashley chuckled.

Jane had always admired Ashley's adventurous nature, although it made her somewhat uncomfortable at times when she expected Jane to match her courage. There are some things that Jane would have never done without Ashley's insistent encouragement. She seemed to be willing to face pain, danger, or any uncertainty head on, which made Jane nervous about Ashley's decisions to do things sometimes. Jane supposed that she learned that from dealing with her mother's mental illness. Jane's Aunt Julie, Ashley's mom and Jane's mom's sister, had been unpredictable and even scary at times for as long as Jane could remember. Ashley grew up never knowing what she might do next. Jane couldn't imagine what that was like to be around all the time.

Ashley's father, Jane's Uncle Scott, was an architect and traveled fairly frequently, and Ashley had always taken care of her mother while he was gone. Luckily, they found the right medicine and Aunt Julie had been sticking with it for several years, which finally allowed Ashley the freedom to be able to go away to college.

Ashley opened the back door, and Edward tried to squeeze through it. Ashley nudged him gently back into the kitchen. "You stay here, boy, and guard the house." She gave Edward an affectionate squeeze around his neck.

"Bye, Edward," said Jane as she patted him on the head. "You be a good boy. Thank you for protecting us." Edward wagged his tail and whimpered, then sat down by the door.

The girls looked around as they crossed the driveway to the back of Bob's house. There was a screened-in porch in back that led to the back door. Jane cupped her hand over her face to peer through the window to see if someone was in there. "Do you see anything?" asked Ashley.

"No, nothing interesting," said Jane, as she stepped back from the window. "It doesn't look as though anyone is here."

"Oh, look it's open," said Ashley, as she gently pushed open the door. "I guess he was planning on coming back in a hurry with those paintings."

"Anyone home?" she called out.

There was no answer. Ashley stepped inside. "C'mon, Jane."

"I don't know," said Jane. She could feel the butterflies in her stomach churning at full speed. She tried to swallow, but her throat felt tight.

"He's dead, Jane. He's not gonna catch us. Just don't touch anything and leave any fingerprints. I don't see any cameras."

"Geez, I didn't even think about security cameras," murmured Jane as she crept in behind Ashley and surveyed the room.

"Ewww, what's that smell?" said Ashley, as she put her hand over her nose.

"Smells like a combination of dirty dishes and cheap cologne," said Jane, also covering her face with her hand.

"And cigars," Ashley added, as she peered into the kitchen. "Looks like he hasn't cleaned lately."

"I guess he didn't have a decorator, either," said Jane. "But he has some nice furnishings. The question is whether they belong to him or not. Look at this vase. It looks expensive, but doesn't look like something he would own."

"He has a few nice paintings he might have been thinking of hanging on the wall." Ashley pointed to the corner of the room, where there were four paintings leaning against the wall.

"That's interesting," said Jane. "But he's lived here for a few years. Most people who have paintings would actually hang them on the wall. I wonder who really owns them."

Ashley started looking around the room. She opened some drawers using the end of her sleeve so that she didn't leave any fingerprints. She also looked around on the shelves. "No photos at all of family or friends. Do you think he had any?"

"That's kind of odd," replied Jane.

"This is interesting. I found a notepad here by the phone. It has a phone number and address on it. I wonder who Sheila Radford is." Ashley pulled out her phone and took a picture of the information on the notepad.

Jane edged towards the back door. "I don't see anything, Ash. Let's go."

"Wait, not yet," said Ashley as she continued to look around. She opened a roll-top desk with her sleeve pulled over her hand, and began to rifle through what looked like Bob's monthly bills.

"Utilities, phone, a letter from the IRS, insurance bills," said Ashley. "I wonder what he's insuring."

Ashley started to read the insurance bill. A car door slammed outside. Then another one. Maybe two. "What was that?" said Jane. "I heard car doors."

Ashley looked up to peer out the front window. "Whoopsie. We have company. One cop car and two other dark sedans. Okay, I'm coming," she said, as she quickly glanced around the room one last time. She stepped quickly out the back door behind Jane.

The girls heard a woman's voice, as well as some men talking, as the visitors were stepping up to the front porch. From the backyard, Jane peered around the side of the house. "Coast is clear." she said. They tiptoed fast across the driveway until they were safely hidden from view.

Edward wagged his whole body and started jumping around, as he greeted them at the back door of Jane's grandparents' house. He acted as though he hadn't seen them for years. "Hi, sweet boy," said Jane, as she tried to give him a pat, while he leaped around them and licked her hands. She wiped her hands on her pajamas and headed to the front window to see what was going on next door. The three cars were still sitting in Bob's driveway.

"They must all be inside. I don't see anyone out there."

Edward followed Ashley into the living room and laid down at her feet. She rubbed his fur around his neck. "You're a good boy." His wagging tail thumped loudly on the floor.

She turned to Jane. "They'll probably be a while, if they're snooping through the house looking for clues. We should call this number I found by the phone and see who answers. It says Sheila Radford. Maybe she is Bob's girlfriend."

"I can't even picture what his girlfriend would look like," as she thought about her impression of Bob. "He was kind of creepy. Maybe we should look up the address or number first and see if we can get any other information," replied Jane. "The address is in New York City. I'll get my laptop."

Jane headed down the hallway and grabbed her laptop from her bedroom. She came back to the living room and sat down. She pulled up a search engine and entered the phone number. "The phone number looks like it's for an art gallery called Black Starling NYC Gallery, in the Chelsea area. Now we're getting somewhere."

"Call it," said Ashley. "See if you can find out what Bob was up to."

"Not so fast," said Jane. "I'm not sure what to say. Let me think a minute."

"I can call if you want," Ashley offered.

Jane hesitated. "I can do it. I just need a minute to think about what to say."

"You should probably call from your grandparents' private landline," suggested Ashley, "so hopefully the number won't come through to the gallery."

"Good idea," said Jane.

Jane felt the butterflies returning to her stomach. She took a deep breath and pressed the number into the phone. "Black Starling NYC Fine Art Gallery," someone answered.

"Can I speak to Sheila Radford?" asked Jane.

"Yes, that's me. How can I help you?" said Sheila.

"Hi, I was given your number by Bob Sheppard."

"Oh yes, Bob. Are you bringing the paintings he wanted to sell? "

"Did he say which ones he was bringing?" Jane inquired.

Sheila's friendly tone suddenly changed. "Why are you asking?" asked Sheila.

"Oh, I was just helping him sort some things out, and he had several different ones. I was starting to get confused as to which was which," said Jane.

"Well, he didn't actually say specifically which ones. He was just going to bring them here. I thought he was planning to bring them himself."

"Oh, well he is, but he was um…. detained, and I was helping him sort things out," said Jane.

"Why are you calling? Are you bringing them for him or what?"

"Actually, I also have a couple of paintings to sell, which is why I'm calling. Bob suggested I call you. I hope that's okay."

"Well, you can bring them by here on any weekday between 8 and 5 and I'll be here to evaluate them. Bob can give you the address."

"Okay, thank you," said Jane. "I can probably …" She heard a click as Sheila seemed to have abruptly hung up while Jane was talking.

"Well, he was definitely gonna sell some paintings in New York," said Jane. "I assume they were my grandparents' paintings, and maybe the ones stacked in the corner at his house. I wonder if he knew about the one in the secret room, or if the bookcase just happened to get pushed open because of the fight in the living room. I'm kind of thinking he was going after Sandpipers by the Sea - the one over the fireplace, since it was hanging crooked."

"I think it was awfully coincidental if he wasn't after the one in the secret room. We would have never found it if the bookcase wasn't left slightly open," Ashley replied.

"That's true," said Jane. "Maybe he was after it. But I wonder how he knew it was in there. Do you think Grandma or Grandpa would have any reason to have shown it to him?"

"I have no idea," said Ashley. "I thought you said they didn't seem to like him that much."

"That's true, too," said Jane.

"I could take the one in the secret room to New York and get the lady to evaluate it."

"I don't know," said Ashley. "If the lady was gonna buy stolen paintings from Bob, she may not be someone you want to tangle with."

"Maybe she didn't know they were stolen," said Jane thoughtfully.

"Or maybe she did, and she had bought stolen items from him already," said Ashley.

"Hmm, maybe," said Jane.

"You should probably take some photos of the paintings he was trying to steal and see if she will evaluate those. Leave the secret painting here and don't let her know about that one. We need to learn more about it."

Ashley didn't usually slow down for much of anything, so Jane took her words of caution seriously. "You're right. It could be really valuable, so maybe I should just keep it hidden. I guess I should do some research and see what I can find out about it. I really should find out more before asking someone else to evaluate it, whether or not they are trustworthy."

"Good thinkin'," nodded Ashley.

"I'm gonna get dressed and eat breakfast and head to the library. Do you want to come to the library with me, Ash? It opens at nine o'clock on Saturdays."

"Not really. But I suggest you take a picture of the paintings to take with you," she replied. "I'm heading for the gym to do some lifting. I have to keep my workouts on schedule while I'm staying here. Edward will guard the house."

Just then, Edward heard his name and jumped up from where he was sleeping by Ashley's foot. He started licking her hands and wagging his tail. "Sorry boy, you can't come with me. You'll have to stay here and guard the place."

"Good idea," said Jane. "Come with me to the room."

"Okay," said Ashley. Jane pulled open the bookcase in the living room and Ashley went in first and turned on the light. "Get some photos of that label that's on the shelf below it, too. Maybe those numbers mean something."

"Yeah, okay," agreed Jane, as she took out her cell phone and snapped a few photos of the painting.

"Got it," said Jane. She stepped back out into the living room. Ashley turned off the light and helped Jane close the bookcase.

CHAPTER SEVEN

RESEARCH WITH NATE

AS JANE HEADED out the door, she called out, "I'm leaving now," to Ashley.

"Don't forget to stop at Jack's Running Store on the way home and get some running shoes," yelled Ashley from the living room.

"Uh, sure thing," yelled Jane. She realized Ashley must be serious about the running. Jane patted Edward good-bye and headed out to her Jeep Cherokee, Bernice. Just before she pulled out of the driveway, she spotted Angela Mott, the real estate lady, driving by. Jane assumed she was showing the house down the street again. She was relieved that Angela didn't come back. She didn't like having to tell anyone her grandparents weren't home.

Jane wished she could be as bold as Ashley sometimes. She didn't seem to let anything keep her down. Jane was really happy to have her back in town for good after four years away at college. The timing was good with her grandparents away. She didn't know who else she could call when a dead body might show up in the living room.

Jane arrived at the West Midland Library and parked in the back of the building. There was something about the library that was always exciting to Jane. The historical sign that stood in front of the library indicated that the building had been a stagecoach stop back in the day. She often wondered what it might have looked like back then.

Jane fondly remembered coming here as a child and how much fun it was to pick out books. Her elementary school didn't have a library, so her class would walk to the library from the school. It felt like a grand adventure. Then the teacher would let her pick out three books to take home. Since borrowing was free, so she could pick anything she wanted. She wondered sometimes if other kids had remembered it the same way.

Jane entered the library and looked around. She smiled as she immediately felt comforted by the woody, earthy aroma that she loved so much, reviving the memories of her many previous library visits. The arched windows of the building always got her attention. It was obviously an old structure. The beautiful architecture looked as though it must be hundreds of years old. There was a doorway to the backroom that had a wooden clock built right into the frame that was magnificent. Jane had never seen anything like it anywhere else.

Jane wasn't quite sure where to begin, as she had never done this kind of research. She walked up to the desk. A young college-age man, neatly dressed in a light blue button-down shirt with a collar and jeans was standing at the desk.

"Hi there." Jane smiled at the young man.

"Hi, my name is Nate. How can I help you today?"

"I am doing some research on a painting," said Jane. "Can you help me get started?"

"Sure," said Nate with a smile. "In fact, I just finished my Masters' degree in Library Science, so you've come to the right person."

"Perfect," said Jane, "because I have no idea what I am doing."

"You look familiar," said Nate. "Do we know each other?"

"I'm not sure," said Jane. She looked into his ocean-blue eyes and admired his dark wavy hair. He looked familiar, but Jane wasn't sure where she might have seen him.

"Do you have any brothers or sisters?" asked Nate.

"Yes," replied Jane. "I have a brother, Michael, in the Marines. He's stationed overseas right now. I haven't even seen him in three years.

"I probably don't know him. But I have a younger sister, Lois. Lois Hensley. She is a sophomore at West Midland High School. Do you know her?"

"Hmm. Does she play softball?" asked Jane, thinking maybe she remembered her.

"Yes, in fact, she does," replied Nate with a smile.

"Ah, that's it. My friend Rachel plays softball. I've

seen you at her games. I've attended many of Rachel's games to watch her play, and I've seen you there on the bleachers."

"That's it," said Nate. "I remember you from there. Now that we have that figured out, how can I help you with the painting? What do you know about it?"

"Nothing really, but I have a photo of it," she said as she pulled out her cell phone.

"That is a good place to start," said Nate. "Maybe we can get the name of the artist. Do you know if it's oil, acrylic, or watercolor? Or is it a print?"

"It's definitely not a print or watercolor, but I'm not sure if it's oil or acrylic. Probably oil, because I think it's really old."

"Sometimes it's difficult to distinguish between a print and original," said Nate. "Just because it's old doesn't necessarily mean it isn't a print. The offset printing press was invented in 1905, so they have been able to make some nice photomechanical reproductions of original paintings since that time. Sometimes you need a magnifying glass to check the brush strokes to help determine the difference."

"It might be older than that," said Jane. "But I don't know for sure."

"Okay, let's see," Nate continued, as he looked at the photo on Jane's phone. "Identifying the artist is going to be our first step. Or if we can find a date to identify the time period, we can research the genre of the artwork and find potential names of artists from that period. It looks like there is a signature, but it's hard to tell whose signature it is. It looks like it says

Gaston Brochard."

"It sounds like it could be French," said Jane. "I don't know if that's helpful."

"There are a couple of ways we can try to identify the artist's signature. First, I'll look up the name. Then there is a database that shows examples of how that artist signs his work, so we can try to match this signature to verify it. I'll have to check if the library has a login for an account for that database.

We can also try to match it to some other paintings by this artist where the signature is identified. Can you send me the photo? Maybe I can crop a copy of it to make it bigger to get a better look at the signature."

"Okay," said Jane. "I really appreciate your help."

"No problem," said Nate. He smiled warmly at Jane. "This kind of research is fun to me. I love all kinds of research."

"I'm glad," said Jane. "I wouldn't know where to look." Jane sent him the photo from her cell phone. Nate was able to make it big enough on his phone to see it more clearly.

"You can stay, or if you want you can come back later and see what I've found."

"Oh, I can stay for a while," said Jane. "I want to learn more about what you're doing."

"Okay then," smiled Nate. "Let's get started." Nate and Jane spent over three hours researching the painting. She looked at many images of paintings and learned a lot about different artists and the differences in style. In between, Nate had to wait on some other people, which took longer. Jane didn't mind. She really enjoyed what she was learning, and she was enjoying spending time with Nate. His dark wavy hair and friendly smile made her feel comfortable working with him. He also smelled really good, and she liked it that he was smart.

"Now that we identified the look of Brochard's signature, we can look in the Art Loss Register and see if any of his paintings may have been stolen at some point," said Nate. "Stolen art has been a big problem for many decades, especially during World War II, when the Nazis stole a large amount of art from family homes during the invasion of neighboring countries, such as Belgium, Austria, Poland, Italy and France, among others.

There are many items that still have never been found or returned to their rightful owners. And many private owners have bought items more recently that they had no idea were stolen. That's why they created the Art Loss Register. It's the largest private database of stolen art, collectibles, and antiques."

"Wow," said Jane. "I had no idea this was such a big problem."

"Oh, yeah," said Nate. "Even the Mona Lisa was stolen right out of the Louvre Museum, but it was returned after being lost for two years." He paused for a moment. "Imagine how bold someone would need to be to steal such an important and famous painting right out of the museum. Just be aware, if someone tries to sell you the Mona Lisa, don't fall for it." Nate laughed.

"Got it," replied Jane. She chuckled at Nate. "I

guess once they stole it, they must have realized it would be difficult to sell."

"The database helps potential buyers answer some questions about past ownership or find further documentation to help minimize the chance that they are buying a previously stolen item," said Nate. "Even the seller may not know it was previously stolen, but it is their responsibility to verify provenance, too."

"What's providence?" asked Jane.

"Provenance." Nate corrected her. "That's the history of ownership. It helps to determine and verify how the painting was sold or given to other people after the artist originally created it," he explained.

"To make sure you're getting an item with a good title, you would need to request a complete list of owners, starting with the artist. If there is a gap in ownership, that might be a point in time when an item was stolen from its rightful owner."

"That sounds complicated," observed Jane.

"People have to do it all the time," said Nate. "Some works of art sell for significant amounts, so you wouldn't want to buy something for a lot of money that you later have to return to its rightful owner.

However, it can be time consuming, and records of ownership are often incomplete. There are often gaps in time with no information. Many of the archives have been damaged over time and in wars, and sometimes galleries might not have preserved the records of their sales and purchases when they close for good. A piece may be part of a collection, and might have been documented as a whole, and sometimes an item is sold out of the collection. This can make it difficult to track down. But we can try – it'll be fun. We won't know until we start digging."

"I'm glad you feel that way, Nate. It sounds overwhelming. Thanks." Jane smiled.

Nate continued working on the library computer as they talked. "And it looks like this one is not listed as stolen," Nate announced. "So that's a relief, right?"

"Yes, I guess that's good," said Jane. "Geez, look at the time. I have really taken up too much of your time today. I really appreciate your help."

"I was happy to help and it's my job, so don't feel bad about it. I'd love to see the actual painting sometime."

"Oh, well, uh, you could stop by the house and see it. You can even stay for dinner, if you want. My cousin Ashley and I are… well, I … am planning to throw together a pizza. Ashley doesn't like to cook. It'll be fun and maybe help pay you back a little for all of your work today."

"Sounds good," said Nate. "I'll be off work at 6:00, if you want to text the address to me."

"Okay," said Jane. "I'll see you soon."

Jane started humming and singing with the radio on her drive home. She was feeling relaxed for the first time in a couple of days, and hopeful that Nate would be able to help her find out why the painting was hidden in a secret room. She was looking forward to seeing Nate again.

When Nate arrived, Ashley opened the front door.

Edward greeted Nate by licking both of his hands and wagging his tail vigorously. Nate seemed to enjoy the canine attention and reciprocated with affection toward Edward. "Hi, I'm Ashley." Ashley leaned forward and extended her hand to shake Nate's.

"Oh, hi there. I'm Nate." He tried to match Ashley's grip, which was stronger than he expected. He didn't want her to think he was a weakling.

"C'mon in," said Ashley. She motioned him inside. "I heard you've been doing a lot of research for Jane today."

"It was fun, really. It helps pass the time at work to do something interesting, and I find research to be thought-provoking, and even challenging at times."

"To each his own, I guess," said Ashley. She shrugged her shoulders. "Jane is in the kitchen, tossing a pizza into the oven. Well, not exactly tossing it." She laughed. "But she'll be out in a minute. Have a seat," she said, as she gestured toward the living room.

"Thanks," said Nate.

Jane smiled as she entered the room. Her eyes sparkled when she saw him. "Hi Nate. Dinner will be ready in about 20 minutes. Do you want to see the painting now?"

"Sure," said Nate. "It would be great to see the real thing."

"I don't know why, but I feel like I can trust you enough to take you into the room where we found the painting. I kind of want to leave it in there and not disturb it. You have to promise not to tell anyone about this, though."

Nate looked puzzled. "I'm not sure what you mean, but sure, I promise. Boy Scout's honor." He held up the three-finger Scout salute.

"Were you a Boy Scout?" asked Ashley.

"You better believe it. Eagle Scout." Nate smiled proudly.

"That's impressive," said Ashley. "I heard that you have to do quite a bit of achievement to become an Eagle Scout."

"Yes, but I enjoyed every minute of it," said Nate. "I can't imagine who I would be without all of my years of scouting."

Ashley pulled back the bookcase, and Jane went in first this time using the flashlight on her phone. She turned on the light. Nate followed her. "Wow, this is interesting," said Nate. "A hidden room!"

"Yeah, we just found it. Weird, huh?" said Ashley.

"Here's the painting," said Jane, gesturing toward it. It was pretty obvious since it was the only painting in the room.

Nate stepped forward to take a closer look. "The frame looks really old, and let's see if there are any markings on the back," he said, as he gently turned it around to look. "Stamps on the back of the canvas or stretcher bars can potentially identify the suppliers of those materials, which can help identify the country's origin or time period."

"Nope, nothing I can see," he said. "Here is a stamp with few numbers on the stretcher. I'll take a picture and write these down in case they are helpful."

Ashley, Jane, and Nate talked late into the evening

after devouring Jane's pizza. Jane confided into Nate what had happened with Bob and his intention to steal the paintings from her grandparents. "We found the bookcase slightly opened after the police left," said Jane. "We were wondering if he knew it was in here and was trying to steal it. So that's why we wanted to know more about it. We still don't know who killed him, but I know it wasn't me or Rachel. Ashley wasn't here that night."

Nate seemed concerned. "So, it sounds like someone else was in the house, too? Maybe he had a partner and they got into a fight. Is it safe for you to be here?" he said.

"I hope we're okay here," said Jane, nervously. "I'm trying not to think about it too much. We have to find out what happened so we'll know whether someone else was gonna come back. Meanwhile, we have Edward here to protect us. I think you may be right. Bob may have had a partner and they had a disagreement that got out of hand. I'm hoping that was the end of anyone breaking in here. But I still need to know for sure. The police were acting like maybe I killed Bob, which is ridiculous. They said they would patrol the neighborhood and keep an eye out for us."

"We found an art dealer in New York, where Bob was gonna sell some paintings," said Ashley. "But they didn't say which ones he was selling. They may be the two from the dining room that it looked like he was gonna steal."

"That makes sense," said Nate.

"I'd love to go to New York and take some photos

of them and see what they say, but I could never go there by myself, and we can't take Edward for protection," said Jane. "The whole idea of doing that makes me pretty nervous anyway."

"Wow, that's an interesting idea," said Nate. "New York isn't that far away."

"I just don't know how else to find out what's going on," said Jane desperately. "The police were acting like my friend Rachel and I killed Bob, and I haven't heard from them since the other night. I'm afraid that any minute they are gonna show up at the door and arrest me. I thought if we could solve the mystery of why he was in the house and who killed him, then I could sleep at night and stop worrying about it."

"Maybe it's a good idea. I could go with you," said Nate. "I've been there once before and know a little about how to get around. I could use some adventure this summer before I have to work full time. We could drive there in about nine hours."

Jane's butterflies were back to visit. She suddenly felt nervous at the prospect of going to New York City, especially with someone she just met, although she had seen him many times watching his sister play softball on the team with Rachel. But she couldn't think of a better plan. However, her dad would be so worried. But she just graduated high school, and she should be allowed to do things like this. "Let me give that some thought, Nate. It was nice of you to offer."

"Okay," he agreed. "Just let me know if you want to go. We could do it in a couple of days."

"You should go!" said Ashley. "You need to find out what happened here, and Edward and I can hold down the fort. Jane, you can do this."

"I don't know," said Jane. "I'm thinking about it."

The next day, Nate and Jane did some further research. The library wasn't open as late on Sunday, but they were able to discover that the painting in the secret room was probably from somewhere in Western Europe. There were some collections from Europe in one of the museums in New York, but they would need to get a better look at the signatures on the other paintings.

"We could see if we can find any other Brochard paintings in one of the art museums, and also stop by the art dealer with some photos," suggested Nate. "It wouldn't really matter which paintings you use for the photos. We could take photos of the ones that guy was trying to steal, just in case those were the ones they were expecting."

"Maybe," said Jane. "It sounds like a good idea. I'll let you know tomorrow."

Later that night, Jane called Rachel. "Hi Rachel," said Jane.

"Hi Jane, are you okay? Did you find out what happened? My dad keeps asking. He thinks you should come stay with us."

"No, I haven't found out anything yet, but I'm working on it. Do you know Lois Hensley that is on your softball team?"

"Oh, yes, Lois. I know her pretty well. Why?"

"Her brother Nate is helping me do some research

at the library."

"Oh, yes, Nate. I know him pretty well, too. He's really nice. Lois adores him. He's cute, too!"

"Yes, I guess he is. I just wondered what you knew about him."

"Well, he's really smart, too. And he comes to our games a lot, and so do their parents. I think he might still be in graduate school."

"He just graduated. Do you think he's trustworthy?"

"Sure, why do you ask?" Rachel wondered.

"I'm thinking about driving to New York City with him for a couple of days to investigate the paintings that the next-door neighbor was trying to steal from my grandparents. I just haven't known Nate for long. He seems really great, but I wanted to check and see if you knew him well and if you thought so."

"Oh, wow. Okay. I've known him for years and I would trust him," said Rachel.

"Good to know, Rachel. Thanks!" said Jane. "I hope to see you soon."

"Me too," said Rachel. "Be careful, Jane."

CHAPTER EIGHT

NEW YORK CITY

JANE AND NATE took off for New York City early on a Monday morning in Bernice. They decided Jane's Jeep Cherokee was in better shape than Nate's Honda, plus it was more comfortable for the long drive on the highway. They managed to find a good deal on a hotel in the Chelsea area, as they each were paying for a room. Jane's graduation check was already coming in handy. Jane sent a text message to Ashley to let her know they had made it to New York.

```
JANE: WE MADE IT
ASHLEY: GREAT - KEEP IN TOUCH
JANE: K WILL DO
```

Shortly after they arrived that afternoon, they visited the Museum of Modern Art to take a look around. They both really enjoyed it. Jane had learned a lot about art from her grandmother, as well as an appreciation for different types of art. They did not see anything that looked like the painting from the secret room.

Next, they checked the Guggenheim Museum. The architecture of the museum was magnificent. They had high hopes when they saw the iconic building. They learned it was designed by Frank Lloyd Wright, and considered to be one of the highlights of his career. As they roamed the main room, they realized that they were unlikely to find any Brochard artwork in this museum. However, they enjoyed seeing some of the rooms and exhibits before leaving.

There was enough time to visit The Strand bookstore, where Nate had always wanted to visit. They walked for countless blocks to get there, witnessing the energy of urban life with fascination. It was different from their normal environment, like nothing they had ever experienced in Ohio. They finally reached the long-awaited bookstore.

Nate grabbed Jane's hand with excitement as they walked into the store. Thousands of books lined the walls. It was even better than he had imagined. He gazed up at the different levels and around at the walls. There were rows of books from floor to ceiling, everywhere he turned.

Jane took a deep breath. "It smells almost as good as the library," she said.

Nate grinned from ear to ear and his eyes danced, as he turned to look at Jane. "There must be a million books here. I'm not sure where to start."

Jane was astonished by the sight of so many books in one place. "You were right! This place is amazing! I guess just pick a spot." She pointed to a corner. "I'm gonna start down here."

"Sounds good. I'll come find you in a bit," said Nate.

After a solid hour at the bookstore, they stopped into a little pizza shop on the same block and had some delicious homemade pizza. "I'm having fun already," said Jane. "So far, New York isn't as scary as I thought it would be."

"There are a lot of things to see here," agreed Nate. "However, we won't have time to do much."

"That's okay, I can always come back another time," said Jane.

The next morning after breakfast, Nate and Jane walked to the art gallery, as soon as it opened, as they didn't want to waste any time. Another couple was roaming around the gallery when they entered. The woman stopped looking at the painting that was nearest to them and looked up at Nate and Jane. The woman put her hand in front of her mouth and whispered something to the man.

Jane scanned her eyes around the gallery briefly. She was aware of the butterflies in her stomach, as they began to churn again. She spotted a woman who appeared to work there, standing in front of a computer. Jane walked towards her, with Nate following behind her. She was well-dressed and well-groomed, wearing a black skirt, blue blazer and white blouse. She had perfectly-styled blonde hair that reached almost to her shoulders. She wore designer reading glasses and an expensive-looking watch. Jane guessed her to be in her mid-fifties.

"Hello, I'm looking for Sheila," said Jane to the woman.

"I'm Sheila, how may I help you?" replied the woman, barely looking up from her computer screen.

"I talked to you on the phone about a painting I want to sell," said Jane.

"Oh?" she replied, still not looking directly at Jane.

"Yes, I have a photo of it here on my phone. I didn't want to drag it all the way here, without thinking I needed to."

"I can take a look," said Sheila, acting slightly disinterested.

"Here," said Jane, as she handed her cell phone to Sheila.

"Hmmm… I can't really tell much by the photo," said Sheila. "Where is it located? Can you bring it in?"

"Um, it's still at my house," said Jane. "You can't tell anything at all from the photo?"

"Maybe," said Sheila. "If you leave me your phone number, I can call you if I can determine anything, but I'll need you to bring it in," she said abruptly. "Or if it's close by, I can come look at it."

"Oh… okay. I wish I had known that would be an issue," said Jane, a little surprised. "It's at my home in Ohio, so I guess that would be a bit far away. Here's my number." Jane smiled at her as she wrote her phone number on one of the business cards from the counter, and handed it to Sheila.

"Where exactly in Ohio?" asked Sheila. She finally looked up and stared intensely at Jane.

Jane's momentary bravery fell to the wayside. She was suddenly apprehensive at the way Sheila was looking at her. "Well, uh, I guess I'll just have to come back and bring it in."

"Okay, then," said Sheila. She turned and walked away.

Jane was confused by Sheila's response. She shoved her cell phone back in her pocket. She looked at Nate with a shrug of her shoulders, and they left the gallery.

As soon as they were outside, Nate said, "That was a little odd and unexpected, don't you think?"

"You thought so, too?" replied Jane, as they started walking down the sidewalk away from the gallery.

"Yes. She really wanted you to bring it in. But if someone had a really valuable painting, I wouldn't think she would expect them to just lug it around with them. I would think photos would be viewed initially, but she seemed as though she didn't want anything to do with looking at a photo of it."

"Yes, that's what I was thinking too," said Jane, as they walked along the sidewalk. They walked several blocks past bars, restaurants, galleries, and other small shops.

They turned the corner and Nate spotted a small coffee shop. "I need coffee. Let's stop here," said Nate, motioning toward the shop.

"Okay," agreed Jane. Nate opened the door for Jane and they were immediately welcomed by the smell of fresh coffee and relaxing music in the background. "Yum," said Jane. "It smells amazing in here."

They marveled at the array of beautiful pastries in the glass case by the cash register. "I wasn't planning on eating yet, but I don't think I can resist," said Jane. Nate ordered the coffee and a pastry for each of them, which they carried to a table and sat down.

Jane spotted a chair and microphone stand in the corner. "Too bad the musical talent isn't playing while we're here," she said.

"Wouldn't that be nice?" said Nate, nodding in agreement, as he worked on his pastry. "This is delicious," he said.

Jane spotted the same couple from the gallery walking in the door. She was surprised to see them so far from the gallery, and so soon after they had left. She had assumed they would still be looking around the gallery.

"Hey look, those are the people that were in the gallery," said Jane, suddenly feeling uncomfortable.

"You're right," said Nate. "Interesting coincidence." The couple sat down at the next table with their coffee and started up a conversation with them.

"Hi, we saw you in the gallery," said the man.

"Oh yes, beautiful items in there," said Nate.

"Yes, there were," the lady agreed. "I'm Sylvia and this is Jason. Where are you from?"

"We're from Ohio," said Jane. "How about you?"

"We are from New York City, born and raised."

"Oh nice," said Jane. "It must have been an

interesting place to grow up. There are so many things to see and do here. You must love it here if you never left."

"What city in Ohio?" the lady persisted.

"Northern Ohio," said Nate. He winked at Jane. Jane stayed quiet and let him do the talking. She wondered why they were so interested in them.

"Well, nice talking to you, we have to go," said Nate, as he picked up his coffee and stood up.

Jane followed Nate's lead. "Yes, nice meeting you. Bye."

"Well, uh, bye, then," said Sylvia, looking disappointed that they were leaving. The couple also stood up and picked up their cups. Nate gave Jane a funny look. He and Jane started walking out the door of the coffee shop.

"Let's get to the subway," whispered Nate. He grabbed her hand and stepped up their pace until they reached the next subway station. They skipped down the steps to the train, two at a time.

"What's the hurry?" asked Jane, trying to keep up.

"That couple back there was asking a lot of questions. I just wanted to make sure no one was following us," replied Nate.

Nate and Jane visited the Metropolitan Museum of Art with no luck, and then had enough time to see Ellis Island and the Statue of Liberty. They were crossing the street to head back to their hotel, when a car sped up and almost ran them down. Nate pulled Jane back onto the sidewalk. "Geesh," said Nate. "That was close."

"It sure was," agreed Jane, her heart beating wildly. "I think I'm ready to leave in the morning," said Jane. She just stood there for a moment holding onto Nate's arm, trembling slightly.

"Me, too," said Nate. "I can't think of a reason to stay longer."

Back in her hotel room, Jane called Ashley to report on how the day had gone. "Sounds like a bust," said Ashley.

"Maybe so," said Jane. Then she told Ashley about the couple in the coffee shop and almost being run down by a car.

"Maybe I'm just being suspicious of everyone," said Jane.

"Maybe," said Ashley. "But I have some good news! I pressed 125 today!"

"125 pounds?" asked Jane.

"Yes!" said Ashley. "That's my best record yet!"

"Well, congrats," said Jane. "That's like a whole big person. You can lift a whole big person?"

"Apparently, I can!" beamed Ashley. "I bet I can lift you!"

"That's great," said Jane. "I'll feel even safer at home with you and Edward."

"Edward misses you, so get home as soon as you can!" said Ashley. After talking to Ashley, Jane went down to the lobby to find out about check out time. As the elevator doors opened, she saw the couple from the coffee shop! Jane gasped and put her hand over her mouth. She stepped back away from the elevator door until it closed and went back up to her room.

Nate was already in his room, so she sent him a text message to tell him that she saw them again.

JANE: I SAW THAT COUPLE FROM THE
COFFEE SHOP DOWN IN THE LOBBY, BUT
THEY DIDN'T SEE ME.
NATE: WHAT — ARE THEY FOLLOWING US
JANE: MAYBE — I THINK IT MIGHT HAVE
BEEN A MISTAKE TO COME HERE
NATE: WHY
JANE: WE DONT KNOW WHAT WE ARE DOING
OR WHO TO TRUST. I JUST WANT TO GO
HOME. LET'S GET OUT OF HERE EARLY
NATE: K
NATE: JANE — IT'LL BE OK. WE'RE OK.
I'LL COME GET YOU AT 6AM.
JANE: K

Jane then gave her dad a call. "Hi Dad, I'm just checking in."

"Oh good, Janie. How's it going?"

"I drove to New York City with a friend and we are leaving in the morning to come home."

"What? You're in New York? Why?"

"Yes, I'm just letting you know. I'm following up on an art gallery address that Bob had written on a piece of paper to see if I could figure out what he was doing."

"Jane, you should not be doing that. Let the police investigate."

"But I'm afraid they think I did it, Dad. I haven't heard anything from them since that night."

"No, they don't think that. Just come home and be careful."

"I will be home soon. There was a couple in the art gallery that we keep seeing. I don't know if they are following us, but I'm in my hotel room and we're leaving first thing in the morning."

"A couple? Who are they?"

"The lady said her name was Sylvia, and the man is Jason, but I don't know anything else about them. She's about 5 foot 3 with kind of scraggly silver hair down to her shoulders. He is probably 5 foot 9 with darker hair. That's really all I know. We ran into them in a coffee shop and talked to them."

"Well, you be careful," said Jane's dad. "I'll see you soon. Let me know as soon as you get home."

"I promise," said Jane.

CHAPTER NINE

A VISIT FROM DAD

NATE AND JANE checked out of the hotel bright and early and made the drive back to Ohio. They stopped at Nate's house first to drop him off. "Whew, that was a long drive, but I did have some fun," said Jane. "I'm not sure how much we learned though, or whether it was a waste of time. There was no sign of Sylvia and that Jason guy she was with on the way home. I'm relieved about that."

"I think we learned a few things," said Nate. "And we visited some museums, and my new favorite bookstore. That was fun. We also had some delicious pizza."

"Yes, I guess so. Thanks for going with me and for sharing the driving," said Jane as she hopped back into the drivers' seat.

"You're welcome," said Nate. "I'm glad I went. See ya soon," he said as he closed the car door.

Jane pulled into her grandparents' long driveway and around the back of the house. She was glad to be home. She spotted her dad's car parked in front of the garage. *I don't remember him saying he would be here*, thought Jane. She suddenly felt bad. *I bet I worried him.*

Jane dragged her overnight bag through the back door. She wouldn't have to worry about Bob showing up and surprising her anymore. Edward greeted Jane at the door, licking her hands and wagging his tail. "So nice to see you Edward," she said as she gave him a quick hug.

"Dad? Ash?" she called.

"In the living room," her dad replied.

"Hi Dad," said Jane as she gave him a hug. "I didn't expect to see you here," she added. "I hope it's not because I worried you."

"Well, you did worry me, but we need to talk."

"Okay." Jane looked pensive. "What about?"

"I need to let you know more about what's going on." He seemed anxious as he looked around the room.

"Do you want me to leave?" asked Ashley, as she started to stand up.

"No, Ashley, I want you to hear this too." Ashley sat back down.

"I did not know that you were going to take off to try to investigate Bob's murder," he began.

"I'm so sorry, Dad." Jane bit her lip. She lowered her gaze away from her dad. "I didn't mean to worry you," she said in a low tone.

Jane's dad continued. "I know that, Janie. However, it's not something I would have guessed you would do. As you know, I work in Washington, D.C. But what you don't know, is that I work undercover for the FBI. I did not want you to worry about me, so I did not share this with you before now."

"Wow, Uncle Bill! I had no idea!" said Ashley. "That's really cool!"

"And you can't share this information, either of you." He gave them each a stern look and pointed at both of them.

"Right, my lips are sealed," said Ashley. "Edward, too." Edward whimpered and laid his head on Ashley's foot.

"Mine too," said Jane.

"After your mom died, I went to work in a job where I could stay home more and look after you. But then your grandparents retired and were more available, so I went back to my FBI job, because I really love this kind of work and I missed it."

Jane smiled sadly.

"I work for the Art Theft division and we've been investigating a global art theft ring. Coincidentally, it turns out that Bob was working with them, well, not with them exactly. He was working as an insurance claims adjuster, and he discovered how valuable works of art can be. So, lacking any integrity, he started stealing artwork and fencing it through local resources."

"I knew he was a weasel!" said Ashley.

"We've been investigating for a while, and one of

the galleries in New York has been a contact through which art works have been transferred to this global art theft group. It's changed names a few times but it is run by a woman named Sheila Radford. Bob was observed visiting the gallery on several occasions carrying paintings in, and leaving the gallery empty-handed."

"Uh oh," said Jane.

"Uh oh is right," said Jane's dad.

"The problem is," he continued, "that there are people willing to buy stolen art for their private collections, just as there are people willing to steal it and sell it to them. Many of them don't know the pieces they have purchased are stolen, but some do.

Aside from the market value of the paintings, many of them are invaluable historically and culturally. There are a large number of art pieces that were looted during World War II, and never returned to the rightful owners, as well as art that was stolen from museums and individual homes at other points in time."

"World War II?" asked Jane. "Wasn't that seventy or eighty years ago?"

"Yes, it was. And there are still many items missing today. Our team has been surveilling Bob for a while, too. I know your grandma has some paintings that are somewhat valuable in the house, and I didn't know if he would make any attempts to steal them while your grandparents are gone, so my team has also been watching your grandparents' house, too."

"Grandma does love her art. You've been watching the house? For how long?" asked Jane.

"Since your grandparents left. I wasn't so worried about your safety with your grandparents' military background, but I wasn't going to let you stay here without keeping an eye out while they are gone. It's not that I don't trust you, Janie, it's that I didn't trust Bob, and I couldn't take a chance on anything happening to you."

"Oh, okay." Jane was dumbfounded at what she was hearing.

"Now you know why I have to travel so much, and why I'm sometimes out of touch. I worry about you when I'm gone, but I know your grandparents were trained in the military and can take good care of you."

"Oh, yeah," agreed Jane. "I feel safe with both Grandma and Grandpa, since I know they were trained in the Army."

"So," Jane's dad continued, "we were here when we saw Bob break in during the night and we followed him in. It wasn't our intention to kill him, but he pulled out a knife and stabbed my partner. Jim is going to be alright, but it turned into a more dangerous encounter than we intended. Since we are undercover, we couldn't make a big deal out of it and tell anyone we were there.

I took Jim to the hospital and called the police on the way to come to the house. After getting Jim checked into the emergency room, I went to the police station to explain the details of what happened. That's why the police haven't gotten back to you with any more questions. The FBI took over the case, and they know what really happened. I've been up all night handling this mess. That's why I missed your call."

Jane's mouth dropped open. "Wait a minute. So, YOU KILLED BOB?" she asked.

"Unfortunately, I had no other choice," said her dad, matter-of-factly. "I had to protect my partner from his attack."

"I guess," said Ashley, hanging on every word.

"Wow, just wow," said Jane. "I wish I'd known. I wouldn't have gone off to New York trying to investigate Bob. The police acted like they thought I did it."

"I know," said Dad, "and if I had any idea in this world that you would take off to New York and try to investigate, I would have stopped you. These people are dangerous, and I don't want you getting in the middle of all this."

"I get it," said Jane.

"There's more," said Dad.

"More? I don't know if I can handle more." Jane couldn't imagine what else she was about to hear.

"Yes," Jane's dad began.

"The couple you saw in the coffee shop, Sylvia and Jason Mulholland, are also involved in the art theft ring. Sheila sent them to follow you and find out where you live. She immediately recognized that painting you showed her as one that Bob was supposed to bring to her. She may have realized from your area code that you live near Bob. Or maybe she had more information from Bob about where the paintings were. She may have found out what happened to him, and maybe that's why she sent Sylvia and Jason to finish the theft."

"So, you knew who they were?" asked Jane.

"As soon as you described them, I knew who they were. Apparently, they already knew something about where you lived, because they beat you home, and we caught them trying to break in. Edward helped us catch them. We heard him barking before we even saw them slip out of the trees toward the back door, and we were able to catch them. They hadn't even gotten to the door yet. I don't think they expected to encounter a barking dog."

"They were here and you caught them?" Ashley was surprised. "I didn't even know."

Jane's heart beat wildly. "They must have left the night before we did, or maybe took a plane here."

"I guess so," said Jane's dad. "When you told me you thought they were following you, I wondered if they might show up here. Sheila wanted that painting that you showed her on your phone. They told us everything, well, probably not everything, but they did implicate her as the person that was directing their efforts to get the painting."

Jane raised her eyebrows. "Wow, at least I know my instincts about all of them were correct. I'll have to listen to my gut from now on."

"Sheila has been running the Black Starling since the 1990s, and has been dealing in stolen art for probably just as long. Well-dressed and well-versed in the art world, Sheila has a lot of connections with some prominent families and art collectors, and is able to fit perfectly in the world of artists and galleries.

Running a gallery in New York City, she is in the perfect location for her to be in the middle of all these connections."

"She really did look very professional," said Jane. "I just thought she was acting strangely about the photos I was trying to show her."

Jane's dad continued explaining Sheila's business. "Sheila has gained quite a reputation, working with other art dealers and artists, and even donating art to museums. She's been able to fence stolen art with the help of small-time thieves such as Bob and the Mulhollands."

"I guess she fooled a lot of people," said Jane.

"Provenance is sometimes accepted when it shouldn't be. Do you know about provenance?"

Ashley smiled and nodded. "Yes, we just learned about that recently." She gave a knowing glance to Jane.

"Sheila has been able to manufacture documents when she needed to fill in gaps of ownership. But she's been hard to catch. So many people are easily fooled when buying art, that it makes it difficult to prove that she had knowledge and intention to sell stolen items."

"Wow," said Jane. "She really did look like an upstanding business woman. I would have never guessed all this. If I'd known all that, I'm sure I wouldn't have even talked to Bob at all. I definitely never would have gone to New York," said Jane.

"Who knew?" she said as she looked over at Ashley.

Ashley nodded in agreement. "Not me," she said. Ashley hadn't met Sheila, but agreed that they didn't know much of anything about this world.

Jane's dad continued. "Although I wish you had not gone to New York and gotten mixed up in this, you did manage to bring the Mulhollands out into the open where we could finally catch them. We have several charges pending against them. We didn't need to catch them actually doing anything. Thank you for that."

"And they gave us enough for a search warrant. Sheila had a backroom full of stolen artwork, so that'll be difficult for her to explain. Who was the friend that was with you? Rachel?"

"No," said Jane. "It's my friend Nate from the library. He was helping me do some research."

"Oh, I don't know him," he said with a worried expression.

"Don't worry, dad. He was a perfect gentleman. We had separate rooms. His sister plays softball with Rachel. You'll meet him soon, I'm sure. I would have never gone to New York by myself. I promise," said Jane.

"Okay, then," said Jane's dad. "But I don't want you trying to investigate Sheila or the art gallery. Leave that to the experts, got it?"

"Yes, dad. I get it now," said Jane.

"Your grandparents should be home in a couple more days, so hopefully we can put this all behind us now," said Jane's dad.

"I can't wait to see them," said Jane. "So much has happened during these two weeks."

"I'll say," agreed Ashley.

CHAPTER TEN

GRANDPARENT NEWS

Just then, Jane's dad's phone rang. "Sorry girls, I have to take this," he said. He stepped out of the room, but the girls could still hear his end of the conversation.

"Teaberry here. Yes… What?" He listened for a bit. "Keep me posted, and I mean I want any updates you have."

"Thanks," he said, as he hung up with a frown. He stepped back into the living room. "This day just gets better and better." Jane's dad looked upset.

"Why, what's going on?" asked Jane. "Am I allowed to know?"

"Yes, I'm afraid so. There was an explosion on your grandparents' cruise ship. Several people are missing or dead. They told me that your grandparents are among them."

Jane suddenly couldn't breathe. Her heart sunk to

her knees, which felt like they were going to buckle out from under her. "No, that can't be true," she said, as she sat down in the nearest chair. "I feel like I would know if they died and I don't feel that. No."

"The news is just breaking," said Jane's dad. "So, it's possible that they are just missing and they'll be okay. We have to believe that until we hear otherwise."

"Yes," said Jane. "I'm hanging onto that. I… just… can't… lose them." Jane ran to her room and shut the door. She sat down in her rocking chair, pulled her knees up to her chin, and burst into tears. She couldn't imagine life without her grandparents.

Jane stayed in her room crying until the shock wore off. She then realized that there was no proof that anything happened to them, and she was determined to believe that they were okay, and it would all get straightened out soon. She dried her face and went back into the living room.

"They're fine," she announced. "There is no proof that anything bad happened to them. We will find them."

"I'll stay on top of this, of course, and let you know anything I hear, Pumpkin. I promise," Jane's dad assured her. I guess I need to also tell you that they went on the cruise because they needed to disappear for a few weeks."

"Disappear?" asked Jane, feeling butterflies in her stomach. Her eyes grew wide with uneasiness.

"Yes, they had recently spotted a criminal in Paris who was on the run since they served in the military. They gave his new location to the authorities, who are currently tracking him down. Unfortunately, he spotted them at the same time, and they may need to testify against him. So, the authorities thought it best to go on the cruise to 'disappear' until he was in custody."

"But they weren't supposed to actually be in any danger, were they?" asked Jane.

"No. They were just trying to play it safe until they could catch him," said Dad. "After being on the run all this time, he probably thinks he won't ever be caught. He won't be worried about their testimony until he is apprehended. I think the explosion was probably not connected, but I really don't know much about what happened yet."

"I sure hope they're okay," said Jane.

"Since I'm a cousin from the other side of the family, Uncle Bill," said Ashley, "I was wondering how Jane's grandma knows so much about art."

"Well," replied Jane's dad, "She was an Art History major in college, and she always loved painting and drawing when she was growing up. When she finished college, she served in the Army, where she met Jane's grandpa, my dad. As you probably know, Jane's grandparents both served 20 years in the military. She was in a unit called the Office of Civil Affairs. Her unit was in charge of maintaining relationships with other allied countries."

"Originally, she performed administrative work, but they called on her more and more for her Art History knowledge. She became experienced in assessing art pieces and became quite the expert in this area. There were so many misplaced art pieces in after the war, that they called on her frequently to help them identify them. Do you know much about the Fuhrer Museum?

"No," said Ashley. "I never heard of it."

"Me neither," said Jane.

"When Hitler was invading various countries in Europe in World War II, one of his grand plans was to open a museum named after himself with all the best art pieces he could find. He had his troops plunder and steal art from people's homes as he invaded their countries. These families considered their paintings and sculptures, and such, as a part of their family's history. These items had been handed down from generation to generation. Stealing these pieces from them made the war even more devastating for everyone."

"That's just awful," said Jane.

"A group was created back then called the Monuments Men, whose goal was to discover where these art pieces were hidden. They've turned up in all kinds of places -- homes, museums, and even some underground caves. They helped return them to the families that owned them. There are books and movies that explain all of the work that they did."

"By the time Jane's grandma joined the Army, a lot of the initial work had been done by the Monuments Men, and their responsibilities had been transferred to a unit in the Army. However, even to this day, there are new discoveries being made, as many items have still never been found. Some museums and individual people have purchased some expensive pieces that they didn't know already belonged to a family in

Europe, and had been missing for many decades."

"It must be exciting when they find a painting that has been missing for so long," Jane said.

"Yes, I think it is. It made your grandma really happy when they could reunite a painting or sculpture with the family that owned it. It wasn't easy to track these down, so it was an accomplishment when they could identify and find the remaining family members. Sometimes the provenance had been fudged to make it look like it was on the up and up.

"Wow, that's amazing," said Jane. "So, Grandma's job was to help them identify paintings when they discovered them somewhere?"

"That's correct. It was part of her job to identify these original paintings," said Jane's dad. "Her unit also worked on maintaining beneficial relationships with other countries. When new items were discovered, cooperation between the countries was and still is necessary to facilitate the return of these works of art. Many of the items may have been stolen from one country, but found in a different one."

"Oh, that makes sense," said Jane.

"She was one of the best at what she did, during the time she was serving in her unit. She loves art, and whenever she had the opportunity to afford paintings she liked, she bought them. She hopefully doesn't have anything that was stolen, since she knows quite a bit about verifying their provenance."

"Wasn't Grandpa in the Civil Affairs unit, too? What did he do?" asked Jane.

"Your grandpa was a reconnaissance expert. He led

a team responsible for civil reconnaissance and engagement. They assessed civil networks and worked to defeat possible threats in the civilian world. He met your grandma through his contacts with the office," said Jane's dad.

"That's really interesting," said Ashley. "Maybe they'll tell us more about it when they get home." She looked over at Jane, hoping that would make her feel better.

"I'm sure they have some interesting stories to tell. Well, ladies, I'm going to have to go now. I feel better knowing how well Edward is guarding the house. You might want to straighten up a bit around here. Your grandmother always kept this place neat as a pin."

"Okay, Dad," said Jane. "You're right. Everything was always perfect. Let me know anything you hear about Grandma and Grandpa, promise?"

"I promise I will let you know as soon as I hear anything," said Dad. "I am going to check on Jim at the hospital and see how he's doing. He should be released today or tomorrow."

"Tell him thank you for what he did," said Jane.

"I will," said Dad. "He'll appreciate that. Bye now," he said as he headed out the back door.

CHAPTER ELEVEN

A NEW POINT OF VIEW

"I SHOULD TELL Nate all the updates," said Jane.

"Wait, hold up a sec," said Ashley. "Uncle Bill said we couldn't tell anyone."

Jane thought for a moment. "He said we couldn't tell anyone he works undercover for the FBI, or that Bob stabbed his partner, or that he's the one that killed Bob, so I'll leave that part out."

"So, you'll just tell him that those people came here, and they were arrested?"

"Yes, exactly. And that Sheila Radford is part of a group of art thieves and was working with Bob. I can tell him that much. He's in pretty deep already with that part of our dilemma. He deserves to know that much. I can tell him my dad found out and told me. He doesn't need to know about the FBI's involvement."

"Okey dokey," said Ashley. "That makes sense."

"Now that this is all settled, I was wondering if you ever bought those running shoes?" asked Ashley.

"You're worried about running shoes now?" asked Jane.

"Well yeah. I think a nice run is just what you need right now."

"To answer the question, yes, I did stop and get some shoes. Just as you requested."

"Let's go then," said Ashley. "You're gonna feel great after a run. We won't go far on your first time out."

"If you promise we're not going far, then I'll come. It'll be good to get outdoors for a bit and get some fresh air."

"Go get changed and let's go!" said Ashley. Edward heard Ashley and jumped up and started dancing around.

"Go get your leash," said Ashley. Edward ran toward the door and stood by his leash, which was hanging on a hook on the wall. He jumped around with excitement, bumping his body into the leash.

"Hurry up Jane!" called Ashley. "Edward wants to go now."

"Coming," called Jane, as she hurried down the hallway.

"Grab a drink of water first." Ashley instructed Jane, as she hooked the leash on Edward and opened the back door.

Jane took a few sips of water, and then followed Ashley and Edward out to the driveway and locked the back door. After a little stretching, they were on their way. Ashley started out slowly so Jane could keep up. Edward wanted to run faster and Ashley held tight to his leash to keep him back with them. He caught on quickly that they had a newcomer on their run and maintained the new pace. Ashley led Jane and Edward around the neighborhood for a mile, before they turned around and headed back to the house. Jane was panting hard, but hanging in there.

"Let's stretch a little bit before we go in," said Ashley.

"Okay," said Jane. She was sweating and panting, and was relieved they were finished running.

"That was two miles! Great first time out!" Ashley smiled. "Good work, Jane. I knew you could do it."

"Not very fast, though," said Jane, still out of breath.

"That's okay," said Ashley. "You'll get faster." The trio entered the back door of the house. Edward immediately started slurping up the water in his bowl. Jane filled two water glasses and handed one to Ashley. Jane leaned against the counter and started drinking the other one.

"Thanks Ashley. That was a tough workout, but I actually feel pretty good and really tired."

"I know, right? It's the best workout, and helps you get all the negatives out of your head."

"I do see what you mean," Jane replied, between gulps of water.

"Where's my phone? I need to catch up with Nate," said Jane. She started looking around for her phone.

"Oh, here it is," she said. Jane sent Nate a text message.

```
JANE: CAN YOU TALK
NATE: IM AT WORK YOU CAN STOP BY
JANE: K
```

"He's at the library, so I'll go talk to him there after I get a shower." Jane headed to her bedroom and took a shower and changed. She gave Edward a goodbye hug, and headed off to the library in Bernice.

When she entered the library, she didn't see Nate at the circulation desk. She looked around and saw him standing by a table. Jane walked over, and as she got closer to Nate, she saw a girl sitting at the table talking to him. She immediately recognized Nate's sister, Lois.

Jane was about to step back to give them some privacy, when Nate spotted her. "Jane," he said. "Hi, come on over."

Jane arrived at the table, and Nate said, "I have to go help a patron. Can you keep Lois company for a minute?"

"Sure," said Jane, as Nate rushed off to help someone.

"Hi," said Lois.

"Hi," said Jane. "I'm Jane. You're on the softball team with Rachel. I've seen you play. You're a good player."

"Thanks, I've seen you at the games," said Lois. She averted her eyes and looked down at the table.

"Is everything okay?" Jane asked.

"I just wish high school was over. I'm tired of it." Lois sighed and slumped her shoulders.

"Tired of school in general or something specific?" Jane asked. She sat down at the table next to Lois.

"To be honest, I'm just tired of mean girls." Lois replied, looking up at Jane.

"Oh," Jane nodded knowingly. "I hear you. It can be exhausting sometimes."

"Right?" said Lois. She looked hopefully at Jane. "You've had problems with them too?"

"Oh sure," said Jane. "I think everyone probably has at one time or another. Have you tried ignoring them or avoiding them?"

"Yes, but that doesn't work. And they always seem to have friends with them, to try to scare me even more."

"Yep," nodded Jane. "That sounds typical. Have you told anyone about it, like a teacher?"

"No, what good will that do?"

"I don't know, I guess it depends on the teacher. My coach hasn't been able to do much either. However, I think it can't hurt."

Jane continued. "My grandpa told me that people that bully others are jealous or insecure. However, I don't know how to fix that, because that's on them. But just so you know, you are not the problem. Mean girls are mean because of something wrong within themselves. They always have bully friends with them because they feel weak. That's what Grandpa always says."

"That's kind of an interesting way to look at it," said Lois.

"I don't know if it helps, because I haven't been able to get certain people to leave me alone, either. But don't let any mean girls make you think any less of yourself, because there's nothing wrong with you. They are the ones that need to fix their own problems, whether it's jealousy or insecurity or whatever. And I've seen you play softball and you have some real talent! They're probably just jealous of you."

Lois looked up at Jane and smiled. "Thanks Jane."

Nate returned to the table. "Sorry about that," he said. "Jane, I need to talk with Lois for a few minutes and then we can talk."

"Never mind Nate. Jane helped me out," said Lois, as she got up to leave. "I've gotta go. Bye Nate, bye Jane," she said. She picked up her books and turned to leave.

"Well, okay then if you're sure," said Nate. "Bye."

"Bye, Lois," said Jane, as she waved to Lois. "Nice chatting with you. Let me know if you want to talk any more about it."

"Thanks for whatever you helped her with," said Nate as he sat down.

"She actually may have helped me see something differently," said Jane. "Do you know how you can know something, but you don't really know it until you tell someone else?"

"Uh, I guess. So, what's up?" asked Nate. Jane explained about the couple that was following them and how they were caught and arrested heading toward the back door of her grandparents' house.

"What a relief," said Nate. He looked around and said, "Let's do some research while we talk, since I'm working."

"Okay," said Jane as she followed him over to the computer desk.

"I was looking up that stamp that was on the canvas stretcher of that painting we were researching. It looks like the canvas was made in the Netherlands. So that is likely where it was painted, and the origin of the artist."

"Wow, great," said Jane. "This is a slow process, isn't it?"

"Yes, I'm afraid so," nodded Nate. "But we're making progress."

"I really appreciate it. I'm really curious at this point about this painting and why it's in a secret room."

"Me too," said Nate. "Plus, it's good experience for me to track it down."

"Well, I have to be going. I promised Ashley I'd do my part to clean the house today. Thanks, Nate. Let me know if you find out anything else."

"I will. See ya," said Nate.

CHAPTER TWELVE

THE KEY

JANE ARRIVED HOME to find Ashley and Edward sitting on the sofa together watching Animal Planet. "So, you didn't start cleaning without me, I see," said Jane.

"Of course not, dear cousin," said Ashley with a grin. "I didn't want you to miss anything, and Edward doesn't like to miss Animal Planet if he can help it. I'm ready whenever you are."

"Okay," said Jane. "Give me just a few minutes and I'll be ready. I never know when Dad is gonna pop in and I don't want him to see it messy again."

Jane got out the cleaning spray and furniture polish and some rags. "Is Edward gonna help?" she asked. Jane smiled at Edward. "He can vacuum some of the fur off the sofa."

"He wants to." Ashley grinned. "Really. He promises to stay out of the way," she added.

The girls started cleaning the living room. They

picked up various items and returned them to their rooms. Ashley vacuumed, while Jane dusted. Jane picked up each item on the mantel to dust underneath them. She carefully picked up the mantel clock, so that she could dust underneath it.

"Look, a key!" she said. "I wonder why it's hidden here."

"Let me see," said Ashley, as she turned off the vacuum cleaner. "It doesn't look like a door key."

"No, it looks like it fits a lock or a drawer or something," said Jane. "I should put it back. It belongs to Grandma and Grandpa. I don't think this is a good hiding place."

"Well, yes, but we still don't know ... you know ... we don't know if they are coming back."

"Don't say that," said Jane emphatically. "They are coming back!"

"Jane, they are at least missing… on a boat … in an explosion. I'm so sorry, but we don't know anything."

Suddenly Edward started barking. Then the doorbell rang. Jane peered out the window to see who it was. "It's that real estate lady again. Let's just not answer it."

Ashley said, "But Edward is gonna bark as long as she stands there."

"Oh alright," sighed Jane.

"Don't worry, I'll take care of it," said Ashley. Ashley opened the door.

"Oh, hi," said Angela. She took a step back and looked up at Ashley, surprised to see her answer the door.

"Hello, can I help you?" said Ashley, holding the door open only slightly, while Edward continued to bark. Ashley looked at Angela closely, noting her heavy makeup, perfect hair and long eyelashes.

Angela looked up at Ashley's tall muscular frame, then smiled and blinked her eyes a couple of times. Ashley didn't say anything, waiting for Angela to speak. "I was just checking back to see if there was any interest in selling the house," said Angela, smiling and trying to make herself heard over the barking.

"Um… no, there isn't," said Ashley loudly over the barking.

"Well, uh, thank you, here is my card again in case you change your minds," said Angela, as she handed Ashley another business card.

"Thanks," said Ashley. "Bye now," she said as she shut the door and locked it.

"Thanks Edward," said Jane to the dog. She patted him on the head.

"Let me find your treats," said Jane. Edward followed her into the kitchen and sat obediently for the treat.

"Good boy!" said Jane as she tossed him the doggie treat.

"Who was that?" Ashley asked as she wandered into the kitchen.

"That was some real estate lady who wants to sell the house. She said she had a buyer that was interested," replied Jane. "I'm glad she didn't ask any more questions. I didn't know how to get rid of her."

Ashley laughed. "Well, it's hard to make your pitch

over barking."

"Okay, well, back to cleaning I guess," said Jane as she headed back into the living room.

"Let's find out what the key fits," said Ashley.

"I don't know," said Jane. "That feels like an invasion of their privacy."

"But maybe it will help them," said Ashley. "We don't know exactly what's going on and your dad said he wasn't sure of it all either. Maybe we'll find something that will help them. If it isn't too late, that is. Don't you think that was a lame hiding place? They probably put it there so you could find it easily, in case something happened to them. Or maybe it's not a big deal or they wouldn't have hidden it there."

Jane sighed. "I'm not sure what we could find. But I would do anything to help my grandparents."

"Okay then," said Ashley. "Let's check out some locks with this key."

"Alright," said Jane. "But if I feel like we are stepping over the line of their privacy, I'm stopping."

"That's fair," said Ashley. "But we won't," she assured Jane.

There was nothing with a lock in the living room. They went out to the breakfast room and found one drawer with a lock, but it wasn't locked, and the key didn't fit. "The office," said Jane. "Let's try there."

Jane and Ashley headed down the hallway to the office, with Edward on their heels. "Let's try the desk," said Jane. She tried the drawers but it didn't fit. She lifted the top piece in the center and found a small drawer next to some tiny shelves. The key fit perfectly.

Jane unlocked the small drawer and took out a small book wrapped with a rubber band.

"It looks pretty old," said Jane. She carefully opened the book to find a lot of numbers and items listed. "This looks like a catalog of items," said Jane. "Three Ships at Sea, Girl with Dog, Field of Lavender," Jane read. "Girl with Dog, that's you!" Jane laughed.

"It also has the artists' names attached," said Jane. "Here is one by Monet. Here is a Van Gogh. I don't recognize a lot of these names, but then I don't know much about artists. I only know the really famous ones."

"They must be the names of paintings," said Ashley. "I wonder if these code numbers match the tags in the secret room. Let's check it out." The trio headed down the hallway back to the living room. Ashley pulled open the bookcase to access the secret room, and turned on the light. "Read off one of the numbers," she said, "and I'll check the tags on these shelves to see if we have a match."

"Okay," said Jane. "BELG 4139," she read.

"Oh, boy," said Ashley. "Here it is. Read another one."

"FRA 987," read Jane.

Ashley looked around. "Yup, here it is," she said. "I think we found the catalog for the items that were in here."

"Let's try the tag for the mystery painting," said Jane. I'll read it and you see if it's in the catalog."

"MNX 092," read Ashley.

Jane flipped carefully through the book. "Here it is, but there is no name attached to it. There is an address listed here inside the cover. I wonder what that is."

"We should be able to find that using a map app. Let's go back to the living room and look it up on my cell phone," said Ashley.

Jane headed back out of the secret room, and Ashley turned out the light and followed her. She gently pushed the heavy bookcase closed. Ashley and Jane each sat in one of the matching chairs by the fireplace, and Edward settled by Ashley's feet. He laid his head on her foot. Ashley looked up the address on the map app. "Obviously it's in France, by the address," she said. "But I want to find out what kind of building it is."

She pulled up the street view. "It's an apartment building in Paris," she announced.

"Interesting!" said Jane. "Isn't Paris where Dad said that Grandma spotted a criminal? Let me see," she said as she walked over to Ashley's chair and looked over her shoulder. "If it's an apartment, I wonder who lives there."

"Someone that is related to the paintings from the secret room," said Ashley. "Otherwise, why would it be in the book? I wonder how long ago they wrote that address in the book. It could have been 20 years, or last month, for all we know."

"I have an idea. Let's go see it!" said Ashley. "It's in Paris and maybe it will help us figure out why the painting is hidden in that room, or maybe we'll find out more about what's going on with your grandparents."

"Do you think so?" asked Jane. "It's awfully far away."

"Like I said before, why would they put that key in such a lame hiding place? Maybe so you'd find it if anything happened to them," said Ashley.

"That's possible," pondered Jane. "We can see what we can learn from some of the museums over there about the secret painting and the ones named in the book. With a name like Brochard, I think the artist must be French, so they will probably have some other paintings by him in one of the museums there."

"Yes, that seems likely! And we can take some photos of the catalog book with my phone. I don't see any danger in going over there to look around museums. We don't have to talk to anyone. We don't speak French anyway," said Ashley.

"That might be worth the trip," nodded Jane. "I just wish I knew how to help Grandma and Grandpa."

"I don't know what we can do to find out what's going on with them," said Ashley. "However, we would need to do some research about this painting to see if it's connected to them having to disappear."

"I promised Dad I wouldn't investigate Bob and his friends anymore, but this is different, right?"

"As far as I know," said Ashley, "this has nothing to do with them."

"Go to Paris, huh?" asked Jane as she scrunched her face.

"Why not? It's summer! Let's have an adventure. My parents have lots of frequent flyer miles – we could get free plane tickets. We just need enough for a hotel, but if we share one, that's cheaper."

"I still have money left from my graduation gift from dad," said Jane. "What about Edward?"

"He can stay with my parents. I'll ask them, but they love him and are used to having him around. I know they miss him since I've been staying here. And your dad already solved the case of Bob, so I think it's safe to leave the house empty for a few days. But you need to let your dad know we'll be gone."

"That makes sense," pondered Jane thoughtfully. "I wonder if Nate would want to go."

"The more the merrier!" said Ashley. "Split three ways, that makes our lodging even cheaper."

"Good point," said Jane. "But I was also thinking about his knowledge of research and what he's found so far. It'll be good to have him along."

"I agree," said Ashley. "I'm heading to the gym to lift while you ask him."

"Okay," replied Jane. "Do you have a passport?" asked Jane.

"Yes," said Ashley, "from when I went on that student exchange program in Spain during college."

"Okay, good. I have one, too, from when we went on vacation in Mexico."

"Looks like we're all set. Check with Nate, and I'll see you and Edward later."

Nate was excited at the prospect of going to Paris, especially with a free plane ticket and a three-way split on a hotel room. How else would he afford it?

Jane's dad wasn't thrilled at the prospect of Jane

leaving the country, but he didn't know a better time for her to go sightseeing with her cousin. He thought it might help get her mind off the break-in and her worries about her grandparents. He thought it would be good to get her away from her grandparents' house for a few days.

Nate couldn't go the next morning, because he first needed to get someone to take his place at work. So, they booked a flight for the morning after that.

CHAPTER THIRTEEN
PARIS ADVENTURE

"RISE AND SHINE, cousin," said Ashley, as Edward pounced on the bed next to Jane.

Jane opened her eyes slightly. "My alarm hasn't gone off yet. I don't have to get up until 3:30 AM."

"But it's about to!" said Ashley with excitement. "There it goes!" she said, as the alarm sounded off playing La Batidora.

"Nice wake up tune," said Ashley. "I like it," she said, as she started salsa dancing around the room.

"Ugh, it's so early," said Jane. "How are you always so wide awake early in the morning?"

"I don't know. The sooner we get to the airport, the sooner we get to Paris," she said. "Plus, we need to drop Edward off at my parents' house and pick up Nate."

"Okay, I'm up. Are you sure we should do this?" said Jane as she sat up in bed, rubbing her eyes.

Edward ran into the room and leaped onto the bed. He started licking her hands and face.

"Okay, that helps," said Jane. "I'm awake, boy. Yuk. Thanks." She patted him on the head.

"Yes, we do." said Ashley. "We need to find out who lives in that apartment to help your grandparents."

"I can't believe we're going to Paris. I didn't know if I ever would get to go there," said Jane.

"Yep, we're going, thanks to my parents and the free miles they gave us," said Ashley.

Jane got up and showered. She got dressed and put the last of her items into her backpack. "Okay, I'm ready." Jane yawned as she hauled her large backpack to the back door. Ashley's backpack was already sitting there.

"Is that all you're taking?" asked Jane. "This looks like it doesn't hold very much."

"That's all I need," said Ashley. "A couple of pairs of shorts and some running shoes. It's summer. We'll just be there a few days."

"We're gonna really stick out as American tourists," chuckled Jane.

"Yep, we are. Let's go," said Ashley. She donned her hoodie and opened the back door to the dark night and the sound of crickets and frogs singing loudly. The competing hum of the cicadas in the trees grew louder this time of year, making it sound like a middle school band that had never practiced together. The envelope of darkness and the brisk night air made Jane a little nervous, as they stashed their backpacks in the back of Bernice. Edward jumped into the backseat.

"It feels like the middle of the night. I don't know how anyone sleeps with all this noise outside," said Jane, as she slipped into the driver's seat.

"That's why we keep the windows closed. Off we go," said Ashley, as Jane pulled out.

They pulled up in Ashley's parents' driveway and Ashley's dad was waiting at the door. He yawned and rubbed his eyes. "You could have dropped him off last night, you know," he said.

"But then I wouldn't get to see him this morning before I leave," she defended.

"Okay, I know. He's your best friend," said Ashley's dad.

"Have a safe trip," he said, as he hugged Ashley goodbye.

"I'll see you on Wednesday. Let me know when you get there," he added.

"I will," said Ashley.

The girls then picked up Nate and headed to the airport. "This is going to be fun," said Nate. "Thanks for asking me to go."

"I think so too," said Ashley.

"Agreed," said Jane.

As they checked in at the airport, Jane thought she saw the same guy from the school parking lot in the security line. "There's Brandi Brown's brother again," she said to Ashley, "or whoever it was she was talking to at school. I wonder where he is going."

"Could be anywhere in the world, I guess," said Ashley. "It's just a coincidence that he's here. I hope Edward doesn't miss me too much," she added.

"I'm sure he will miss you, Ash. But we won't be gone long. We can only afford a few days," said Jane.

"True," said Ashley. "I miss him already. I wish he could have gone."

"I'm sure your parents appreciate spending time with him," said Jane. "Think of it that way."

"Yep, sounds better that way," nodded Ashley.

After a long flight, it was the middle of the night when they arrived in Paris. They managed to flag down a taxi to take them to the hotel, just down the street from the Parc du Champ de Mars. Jane gazed out the window, as they rode through the streets of Paris. "We really are far away from home. This is so different," she said. "I love it."

"Yeah," said Nate. "I'm gonna have to come back when I can stay for a few weeks. It looks like there is a lot to see here."

They stepped into the hotel. Jane looked around at the lobby, mostly decorated in white and black, with marble floors and tasteful furnishings. "This is a beautiful hotel," she said. "I hope we really can afford it."

"Welcome to Paris!" said the desk clerk, as they checked in. "I am Michel. Let me know of anything you need while you are here."

"Thank you," said Nate.

The hotel manager stepped out from an office door behind the desk. "Welcome! I am François, the hotel manager. I hope you will be comfortable during your stay. Paris is a beautiful city with much to see. You will enjoy it very much. However, do not carry a backpack or purse. Leave your valuables here," he said. "I am serious. Please be careful."

"Merci," said Nate. "We will." Michel handed Nate the key and the trio headed to the elevator with their backpacks.

"I'm beat," said Nate, as they took the elevator to the room.

"Me too," agreed the girls in unison.

Their room décor was beautiful and there was plenty of space. Jane was amazed when she saw the spacious and elegantly furnished bathroom. "I think I could just live in this bathroom. It's magnificent!"

Ashley and Jane shared a bed, and gave the other one to Nate. They were all weary from the flight, but not sure they could sleep yet, as it was late at night in Paris, but only dinnertime at home. They pulled out the snacks they had, and feasted as best they could.

"I have some almonds," said Jane, "and some chocolate granola."

"I have crackers and some cheese spread," said Ashley. "Hopefully I can find a plastic knife here somewhere. I think I had one," she said as she dug into her backpack.

"I have chocolate covered peanuts and licorice," said Nate. "Luckily, we have a little refrigerator here, so we should get some snacks tomorrow while we are out."

"Did anyone bring an adapter to plug in our phone chargers?"

"I have that covered," said Ashley. "I borrowed one from my parents."

"Great! I don't know what we would do without our cell phones," said Jane. "I didn't even think about it."

"I did a little quick research on the area, and there is a park down the street called Parc du Champ de Mars, so we can grab food somewhere and eat there while we are here, during the daytime, of course. It's right in front of the Eiffel Tower," Nate suggested.

"Aren't you glad we brought him?" said Jane to Ashley.

"Sure, that'll be useful to know our way around a bit. We have an address we want to visit at some point, just to see what it is," said Ashley.

"An address? You don't know what it is?" asked Nate.

"Nope," said Ashley. "We found it in a book at her grandparents' house."

"Okay," said Nate. "We can just find it on a map app."

"That's what I thought," agreed Jane. "I didn't think it would be difficult to find."

Ashley looked it up in the Notes app on her cell phone, where she had stored it earlier. "It's 7848 Rue de Grandemere. Apartment 1B."

"Okay," said Nate. "Give me a few minutes." He sat on the end of the bed and intensely studied his cell phone. "Here it is," he said. "We can take the train to a stop pretty near it. I'll download a Métro map, so we can find our way around the city."

"Perfect," said Jane.

"It looks like we could start with the Musée

d'Orsay and then pass the apartment on the way to the Louvre Museum," said Nate.

CHAPTER FOURTEEN

MUSEUM REVELATION

THE NEXT MORNING, the trio got up later than expected with the time difference. They went downstairs and asked the desk clerk where they could find something to eat.

"There is a pastry shop at the end of the block," said the clerk. "You could get some croissants or pastries there for petit déjeuner."

"For what?" asked Jane.

"Petit déjeuner… breakfast?" said the desk clerk.

"Oh, right. Perfect," said Jane. "Merci."

"It's getting closer to lunchtime," said Ashley. "Why don't we go to a restaurant for brunch or even lunch, and then we won't have to worry about eating until much later."

"We could stop at a market and get some food, and then we can go to the park that Nate mentioned. Champ de Mars? Was it?" said Jane.

"Yes, that's it. It's right down the street from the hotel," replied Nate.

"I hope it's a decent sized park, because I'm going for a run before I eat. I haven't been to the gym in two days. Who wants to run with me?" asked Ashley.

"I'm good," said Nate. "You go ahead."

"Me too," said Jane. "I didn't bring my running shoes. We'll take our food to the park and you can run around us."

"Okay," said Ashley. "But I'm gonna have you excited about running at some point. I just need to grab my running shoes."

Ashley went back to the room to get her shoes before they left. The trio stopped at the nearby market for some deli meats and cheeses and bread, and drinks. Then they walked down the street to the Parc du Champ de Mars.

"It's beautiful!" exclaimed Jane. "What a nice park."

"And big!" said Ashley.

"It's like we are right in front of the Eiffel Tower. We'll have to get some photos of ourselves here," said Jane.

"This is amazing to see the Eiffel Tower up close and in person after all the photos we have seen all of our lives. Wow!" said Nate.

"Okay, let's get the photos first before I'm all sweaty," said Ashley. They stood in front of the Eiffel Tower and tried to take some selfie photos, but were having trouble getting the whole Eiffel Tower into the photo. Jane asked another tourist to take the photo for them from farther away.

"Merci, thank you," said Jane, as the other tourist handed back her cell phone.

"Got it," Jane said to Ashley. "Now go run! We'll be right here." Jane and Nate found a nice spot in the shade, and set out their lunch options in front of them in a grassy area.

"I'm starving," said Nate, as he started building a sandwich for himself.

"Me, too," said Jane, following suit. Ashley started trotting off and ran laps along the paved areas of the park.

"What's over that way?" asked Jane, pointing towards some buildings.

"That's the military school. They call it École Militaire. It's an active military training center. It was built in the 1700s by King Louis XV. There's a train stop next to it where we can catch the Métro."

"I knew you would know!" said Jane.

Nate and Jane relaxed and ate their sandwiches, while Ashley ran until she reached five miles, according to her GPS watch. "All done!" she said, as she plopped herself on the grass beside Jane and Nate. "Where's the water?"

"Here you go," said Jane. "Help yourself to the food. You must be starving by now."

"I am!" replied Ashley, as she started to make herself a sandwich. They sat and relaxed together in the shade while they all finished eating.

"What do you want to do first?" asked Ashley.

"Let's head for the Musée d'Orsay," said Nate.

"They have a large variety of paintings there. I'm really looking forward to it. Then that apartment building you mentioned is on the way to the Louvre. "

"Sounds good!" said Jane.

As they entered the Musée d'Orsay, Nate shared what he knew about the museum. "They have the largest collection of French paintings from 1848 to 1914, and they also have sculptures and photography. I heard they have some great temporary exhibits, too. Maybe we can find the artist that created the painting in the secret room here. It seems more likely that this might be the right museum."

Jane nodded. "This is a great museum," she said, looking in awe at the walls. "I had only heard of the Louvre, but this museum has a lot of great stuff. I really like Van Gogh and Monet."

"Van Gogh's Starry Night is my favorite. I hope it's here. I would love to see it in person," said Nate.

"Did you see that giant clock?!" said Jane.

"Yes! It kind of reminds me of the clock at the library. This one might be older, but the library clock is really old, too. This building used to be a train station for a long time," said Nate. "They kept the clock when they switched it over to the museum."

"I'm glad they did because it's amazing!" said Jane.

"It is a cool looking building," said Ashley, as she gazed around the room. "Everything looks really old, and a lot cooler than any of the buildings at home. It feels like we're in a palace or something."

"Funny you should say that, because before it was

a train station, this was a government palace in the 1800s. But there was a fire that destroyed most of it. They rebuilt it and made it into the train station around 1900. It wasn't a museum until the mid-1980s, when the Louvre had so much extra artwork that they needed another museum to display some of it."

"You sure know a lot about this place for being in a foreign country," said Ashley.

"I looked it up before we got here," said Nate. "I work in a library. That's kinda what I do."

Ashley laughed. "I guess it is."

"I really would like to see some of the impressionists while we're here," said Jane.

Ashley looked at the guide. "I think that's on Level 5. Should we start there or work our way towards it?"

"Wait. Stop. Look over there," said Nate, as they walked around. "Do you recognize it?"

Jane gasped. "It's the painting from the secret room! Exactly!"

"It looks like it to me. Did he paint two of them? Let me check out the signature," said Nate as he walked closer to the painting.

"It's the same painting," he said. "It says 'Woman with Red Flower,' and the artist is Gaston Brochard."

"I don't get it," said Jane.

"I don't either," said Nate.

"Let's get a photo of it, along with the description next to it." Jane pulled out her cell phone.

"Good idea! Also, let's note where exactly we found it, so we don't forget." Nate looked around. "Look! Here are more paintings by Brochard. Woman with Butterfly, A Walk in the Lilies, and Goddess in Blue. All by Gaston Brochard."

"Bingo! We found him," said Jane. "I'm not sure what we know at this point, but at least we found the artist. I didn't think we'd find the exact same painting."

Nate spotted a docent giving a tour. "Let's go listen," he told the girls. They stepped into the tour group.

When the docent asked if there were questions, Nate asked, "Is the artist Brochard well known?"

The docent replied, "Yes, this artist is known in certain circles. There are a limited number of these original Brochard paintings. A couple of the original works had gone missing during World War II. As far as I know, they are accounted for at this point. Brochard's works are quite valuable and well known."

"Where could I find more about this artist?" asked Nate.

"There may be a book or two in the museum gift shop, and there is a bookstore around the corner on Rue de l'Université that has many art books," said the docent.

"Merci," said Nate. He turned to the girls and said, "We need to check the gift shop and that bookstore when we leave here."

"I think we found our next clue," said Jane, "so let's go see the Impressionists, and then I'm ready to check out the gift shop and get out of here."

"Agreed," said Ashley.

After looking at some of the Impressionist

paintings, they roamed around the gift shop. Jane looked through the books that were offered. She didn't find anything about Brochard, but Nate bought a pretty scarf for his little sister.

"Ready to go?" asked Nate.

"Yes," said Ashley. "Let's go to the bookstore." The trio started walking to Rue de l'Université.

Nate was excited. He loved visiting bookstores. He grinned with anticipation as they approached the bookstore. "We're here!" he exclaimed. "I wasn't sure I'd get to visit any bookstores while we're here and I was very curious to see what they are like in France."

They looked around at the books and Nate found one that included Brochard. "Here Jane, let's get this book," said Nate. "There are several paintings by this artist in it."

"Great," said Jane. "I'll pay for it." They left the bookstore and headed down Rue de l'Université.

"Let's go to the Louvre now," said Jane.

"Before we go there, can we do something else first?" said Nate. "I mean, I know that's kinda why we're here, but there are two things I want to make sure I see while I'm here."

Ashley nodded. "Okay, lead the way."

Nate looked at the map app on his phone. "It's about a half hour walk from here. We can get a great view of the Seine River while we walk there. We just need to get to the Pont Alexandre III, which is a bridge to cross to the other side. 'Pont' means 'bridge'."

"This view is beautiful," said Jane, as she looked across the Seine River. They took several pictures along the way, while they walked alongside the river. At the end of the Pont de l'Alma bridge, Jane could see they were approaching a large gold sculpture on a pedestal of gray and black marble on a circular platform. It appeared to be sitting by itself, away from any buildings. She wondered what it could be, as it was cordoned off, and there were some bouquets of flowers and posters inside the cordoned-off area.

"Here we are!" said Nate. "The Flame of Liberty, or as they call it in Paris, Flamme de la Liberté. I just found out about this last year. This gold-leaf-covered flame is a replica of the flame that's on the Statue of Liberty torch. It's the exact same size."

"It's a symbol of friendship between France and America," added Ashley. "I learned about this in one of my classes at school."

"Right, good Ashley! See, you know about some of these things," said Nate. Ashley smiled proudly.

"It was a thank you gift for restoration work done on the Statue of Liberty. It's not as old as most of the landmarks in Paris," Nate continued.

"Wow. I didn't have to climb up the lady to see the giant flame. It gives me a better idea of how large it actually is, seeing it up this close. Pretty cool," said Jane.

"Also, the tunnel underneath is where Princess Diana died in a car crash," said Nate. "Very unfortunate. Because it happened in this location, this sculpture has become a sort of memorial to Diana, Princess of Wales. She was beloved by many people around the world."

"I didn't realize that. I just thought the flame was pretty cool," said Ashley, shrugging her shoulders. "I guess all that happened before I was born." Ashley walked around it to look at all sides of it. She pulled out her cell phone to take a photo.

"Let's walk over to the Place de la Concorde, while we're nearby it. It's over this way," said Nate. He motioned towards it.

"What's that?" asked Ashley, as they all started walking.

"It's where they used to keep a guillotine back in the day."

"Oh," said Ashley. "Is that the one where Marie Antoinette had her head chopped off?"

"Yes, it is," replied Nate. "And so did King Louis XVI, during the French Revolution. But so did many other people that you don't ever hear about. Those were tough times for France. It just doesn't seem real, without actually visiting the place and seeing it up close. I thought it would be cool to see while we're here."

"Here we are," said Nate, as they approached the area.

"You're right," said Jane. "It doesn't seem like a real thing that they would do by just hearing about it. But times were very different back then. Every big city has its ups and downs, especially when the city has been around as long as this one. And now we are standing right here where history was made, hundreds of years later," she said, as she walked towards it.

Nate pointed. "This centerpiece is an ancient

Egyptian obelisk. See this tall thin structure with the hieroglyphics? It's one of two that the Egyptian government gifted to the French in the 19th century."

"Where's the other one?" asked Ashley.

"The second one never made it to France, because it was too large and heavy, so they ended up keeping it in Egypt. The pedestal that it sits on is left over from where a statue of Louis XV used to stand, before it was knocked down during the French Revolution."

"What do all these hieroglyphics mean?" asked Jane.

"I don't know," said Nate. "But I do know that at the top there is one showing the Pharoah on his throne. Reading the rest of it would require a lot more research. Maybe we can find out when we get back home."

"I'm starting to get hungry. Where do you want to eat?" said Ashley.

"I'll see if I can find something on my phone," said Nate. "Here we go. There is a place near here that has crêpes and galettes. We should try it. Hopefully it's not too expensive."

"Sounds good," said Ashley. "Lead the way!"

They walked a few blocks to the restaurant. "Here it is, Poire et Cannelle." Nate pushed open the door and held it open for the girls.

"I like it," said Ashley. "I'm starving!" Ashley and Jane walked in with Nate following.

Jane looked around the restaurant. There was light background music and a quaint feel to the place. The tables were covered in dark green linen tablecloths, and each table had a candle centerpiece. There were a few tables with customers already seated. The aroma of delicious food wafted through the air.

"May we sit at the table by the window?" asked Jane, pointing to a table by the window. The server motioned them towards the table affirmatively without speaking. She set the menus on the table.

"This is so cool." Jane smiled as she looked at the menu. "It's so different from home."

"It sure is," agreed Ashley. "I'm having more fun than I thought I would."

"I hope the server speaks a little English. Do either of you know what a galette is?" asked Jane.

"We shouldn't assume anyone speaks any English. We'll do the best we can by pointing to the menu, I guess." said Nate. "A galette is kind of like a crêpe but made from buckwheat. They can be stuffed with a number of different fillings. I think I'll get one with ham and cheese."

"That sounds interesting and delicious," said Jane. "I'm not sure whether to get that or crêpes. A crêpe with chicken and cheese sounds good."

"I'm getting an omelette," said Ashley. "That's something I can understand." She laughed.

They placed their orders, and it wasn't long before the server delivered their food. Nate's eyes lit up when he saw his plate. "This galette looks delicious," he said.

"It all looks good," said Jane. After they ate, Nate checked his phone as they were leaving the restaurant. "We should probably be getting back to the hotel. It's getting late. The Louvre is closed now. It will have to wait until tomorrow."

CHAPTER FIFTEEN

LOST IN PARIS

THE NEXT MORNING, the trio was up earlier than the previous day. As they stepped out of the hotel into the fresh summer air, Jane could smell the sweet aroma of pastries baking. She gazed up and down the Paris street and tried to take it all in. The charm of the quaint shops, one-of-a-kind boutiques, and the fresh produce and flower stand was nothing like her hometown, and she wanted to cherish the moment and remember it all.

"I can't believe we're in Paris," said Jane, as they started walking. "It never seemed real in the movies and here we are."

"Let's stop at that pastry shop on the corner for some chocolate croissants to take with us," said Nate.

"Sounds good. I can smell them baking from here. Do you have the address to the apartment building, Ashley?" asked Jane.

"Yes, I have it right here on my phone. I'm pulling

up the map now to see how to get there."

"What address?" said Nate.

"The one in the log book," said Jane.

"What don't I know about this apartment building and log book?" asked Nate.

Jane explained. "We found a log book in my grandpa's desk with a catalog of items that corresponds to the tags in the secret room. There was an address listed and circled in the book. It looked important. So, we wanted to come and see what was there."

"What?" said Nate. "You don't know what we might be getting into," said Nate. "This is starting to feel a little unsettling. Jane, we need to be careful here."

"We're just gonna look while we're here," said Ashley. "What could that hurt?"

"I don't know. That's what we thought when we went to New York. I don't think it's a good idea," said Nate.

"It can't hurt to just look," said Jane. Nate shrugged in silence.

"We can take the Métro to get there a little faster," said Ashley. There's a stop up the street here at the École Militaire. "It's just a few blocks from here. Let's stop for coffee on the way."

They stopped in a coffee shop to order coffee. "Three café Americanos, s'il vous plaît? We just want it to go, to take out?" Ashley smiled at the server and held up three fingers. She turned to Jane and held her hand in front of her mouth. "I heard that if you don't say Americano, you just get a little tiny cup of coffee."

"And if you ask for a latté, you'll just get milk," whispered Nate.

"Asseyez-vous," said the server, as she motioned for them to sit down at a table.

"We just want three of them to go, to take out?" Jane tried to explain, holding up three fingers.

"Asseyez-vous," she repeated, motioning toward the table.

"Okay," said Jane. "We'll sit." She smiled and nodded at the server.

They sat at the table and the server brought the three cups of coffee. They stayed to drink it, since they were not served in paper cups. Then they headed out to the street. "Which way?" asked Jane.

"The Métro stop is right here on the corner," said Ashley. Ashley bought some tickets and they took the train to the stop nearest the apartment.

"Turn left, when we get off the train," said Ashley, looking at her map app. When they exited the train, they started walking down the street and had to take a few turns before reaching the address.

"It does look like an apartment building. The one with the red awning over the front door," said Nate, pointing.

"Yes," said Jane. "This looks like the picture Ashley looked up at home. Now what?"

"We should see who lives there," said Ashley.

"What if it's a criminal?" said Nate. "Are you sure you know what you're doing here? Let's be careful after what happened in New York. What aren't you telling me?”

"Nothing," said Ashley. "We found an address in a book at her grandparents' house, and we wanted to find out more about it. I don't know why there would be a criminal living there. It isn't related to Bob in any way."

"As far as we know," said Jane.

"But why?" asked Nate.

"Because," said Jane, "it was in a book that appeared to be a catalog of the paintings that were in the room behind the bookcase. We wanted to know what it had to do with the painting in the room."

"What are you gonna do, just knock on the door, and then what?" asked Nate, seeming annoyed.

"I know," said Ashley, "we'll ask for Jacques!"

"Who is that?" said Jane.

"I don't know," said Ashley. "But we'll get to see who opens the door."

"This is our one chance to find out the name of the person that lives there. Once they open the door and see us, that blows our only chance," said Jane.

"Maybe there is a name on one of the mailboxes. Apartments always have a row of mailboxes in the lobby. Then you don't need to knock on any doors," suggested Nate.

"That's a good idea!" said Jane. They went in the front door of the building and found a row of mailboxes. "Here it is," she said. "Blanchet, it says. So, we have a last name."

Ashley was standing by the door watching the street. "Hey, is that guy watching us?"

"Where?" said Jane.

"Over there in front of that store," she said. "Maybe he's waiting for something. He's just standing there looking at his phone."

"There's another guy by the news box just standing there as well. Maybe we're too suspicious. I always feel like someone is watching me," said Jane.

"Okay, so what's the plan?" asked Nate. "This is making me nervous."

"Ashley will stay down here," said Jane. "You and I will knock on the door and pretend we are married and ask for someone who is supposed to live there."

"Jane, I don't want anything to happen to you… or me, for that matter. I wish you would be careful. We don't even speak French," said Nate.

"I'll just ask if this is the home of someone in particular. Then they will say no, and then we will at least get a glimpse into the apartment and see who answers the door. That's all we need to do and all we really can do. They are not gonna volunteer any information. We have the name from the mailbox. We can research it later."

"Sounds like a total waste of time, but okay," said Nate.

Nate and Jane went up the stairs and knocked at the door. A woman with long red hair, wearing a white satin robe and fuzzy white slippers answered the door. She had a cigarette in one hand.

"Bonjour?" she said as a question.

"Hello, I'm looking for Paul Martin. He is supposed to live here. Is he home?" said Jane.

Nate could see a man sitting on the sofa drinking from a tiny coffee cup. He had dark slicked back hair and dark rimmed glasses, and was wearing an oversized shirt and trousers. He had a large ring on his right hand and bare feet. He peered over the magazine he was reading to see who was at the door.

The lady emphatically said, "Non!" and shook her head, and then shut the door. Jane and Nate could hear her spouting off something in French that sounded like she was annoyed. Then they heard the man respond in a deep voice, but they couldn't hear or understand what he said.

"Okay, then," said Jane as she turned to walk away.

"Let's get out of here," said Nate. They hurried down the stairs.

Ashley was waiting by the door. "Nothing going on down here," she said.

"Let's go," said Jane to Ashley, as she bolted toward the door and pushed it open. The trio left the building. A minute later, the barefoot man from the sofa also left the building right behind them.

"Is there anything else I should know about this trip?" asked Nate, as he tried to keep up with Jane, who was walking a lot faster than she was earlier.

"No," said Jane. "Only some museums to do painting research. Let's go to the Louvre now."

"Good," said Nate. "That is something I look forward to doing. This app says the Louvre Museum is on the Right Bank of the Seine, in the first arrondissement. So, it isn't far from here."

"How do we get there from here?" asked Ashley.

"It looks like we can walk there in 12 minutes, so no need for a bus or train." Nate looked up from his cell phone and pointed. "Turn right at the next block. Then we need to cross Pont Royal."

As they approached the grounds of the Louvre Palace, they all marveled at the impressive structure. Jane gazed up at the palace arches and took photos of some of the detailed work on the front of the buildings. She hoped she could look closer at the photos at a later time, so she could study some of the details. "I don't think I've ever seen anything like this," she said in amazement. "The details on these buildings are incredible. They would never put in the time and effort nowadays to create buildings like these."

"This palace, called the Palais de Louvre, was originally a medieval castle back in 1190," said Nate. "The oldest section that still exists was built in the 1500s. Most of the sections of the current building were constructed in the seventeenth and nineteenth centuries. It's served a lot of different purposes over time."

"What don't you know?" asked Ashley. "You're like a walking encyclopedia."

"A lot," said Nate. "But I knew we were coming here, and I like to know things ahead of time so that I can get the most out of my experiences. The museum takes up most of the palace, but not all of it."

"Jane was right to ask you along." Ashley chuckled.

"Glad I could be useful. What a cool entrance,"

observed Nate. "We need to head to that pyramid over there, and find the queue for visitors without tickets."

"Here we are," said Ashley. "Geez, this place is crowded. I'm not surprised, though. Probably everyone that comes to Paris wants to come here."

They were able to get through the line in about a half hour. "That long line went faster than I expected," Jane observed.

Ashley pulled up the museum map on her phone as soon as they entered the building. "This place is mega huge, so we're not gonna be able to just wander through it. We need to decide specifically where we want to go."

Jane peered over Ashley's shoulder at the map. "Looking at the map, I don't think we're gonna find any Brochards here, but we should look at the gift shop for books before we leave. Let's go see the Mona Lisa first," said Jane.

As they approached the area that houses the Mona Lisa, Jane spotted a large crowd in one area. "What's over there?" she asked.

Nate moved in closer to look. "There she is. It's the Mona Lisa," he said, as he pointed through the crowd.

"Look how small she is," said Ashley.

Jane looked surprised. "No wonder someone was able to hide it for two years. I was picturing something much bigger." Jane stepped back away from the crowd in front of the Mona Lisa, trying to get a better view. A man bumped into her. "Ow," said Jane, as she stumbled forward.

"Excusez moi," he said, and turned away from her.

"Hey, I think that was the guy from that apartment," said Nate. Jane turned around to look, but the man was gone.

Jane stepped in closer to the Mona Lisa. She pulled out her phone and took a flash photo. Security guards immediately approached her. "Come with us," said the man in the security uniform.

Jane looked at the two security guards, a man and a woman. "What?" she asked.

They whisked her away to a nearby office. "We need to see your identification."

"But why?" asked Jane. "And my friends. Where are they? They won't know where I am."

"Flash photographs are prohibited. You have violated the museum rules. We must see your identification."

Jane reached in her small purse for her driver's license. "My wallet is gone!"

"Gone? When do you remember having it last?" asked the guard.

"It was when I paid to get into the museum. Someone must have picked it from my purse in here," said Jane, continuing to dig around in her purse.

"You must provide to us your name and address so we can verify your identity." The guard handed her a pen and paper.

"Okay," said Jane. She took the pen and wrote down the information they requested.

"Wait here," said the guard. Jane sat alone in the office and waited, worrying about what was next. *Are they gonna arrest me?* she wondered. After about 20 minutes, they came back. Luckily in this day and age, it was easy to look someone up online and verify who they are.

"You may leave, but do not take any more photographs. Flash photography is prohibited in the museum."

"Thank you. Merci." said Jane. She left the office and made her way back to the Mona Lisa. She looked around but did not see Nate or Ashley in the crowd. Jane tried calling their cell phones but neither of them answered.

Jane looked around for a bit and couldn't find them anywhere near the section where she last saw them. Jane burst into tears and sat down on a bench with her face in her hands. She didn't want anyone to notice her. *What am I gonna do now? Don't be a crybaby, Jane. Knock it off,* she thought to herself. Jane held tightly to the coin on her mom's necklace and closed her eyes for a minute, hoping her mom could somehow send her a message and tell her what to do next.

She tried sending them both a text.

JANE: WHERE ARE YOU? I'M STILL AT THE LOUVRE. ARE YOU?

Jane sat on the bench and waited ten minutes for a reply, but no one replied. She put her cell phone back in her pocket and did her best to pull herself together.

Maybe they are waiting at the entrance, she thought. *I'll go there and find them.*

Jane wandered around outside near the entrance, looking for Nate and Ashley. They were nowhere to be found. *What could have happened to them?* thought Jane. *Here I am alone in a foreign country and I only know how to say 'bonjour' and 'merci'. What am I gonna do now?*

She dug in her pocket for cash to buy a train ticket, since Ashley had the extra Métro tickets. "Rats, no money!" she said aloud. She pulled up a map app on her cell phone to see where she was. She realized with no money she would have to walk all the way back to the hotel. *Maybe Ashley and Nate will be there*, she thought. *I don't know where else to look for them. But why would they leave?*

Hmmm, what was the name of the hotel? she thought to herself. She had depended on Nate and Ashley to navigate the city up to this point. Now she would have to figure it out for herself. She suddenly felt very alone.

She found the name of the hotel and then found it on her phone app. *It's a good thing I still have my phone*, she thought. She clicked for walking directions and started walking. At first the streets looked familiar as she crossed Pont Royal. Then she found herself on different streets that they had not traveled on their way to the Louvre.

Black clouds began to loom overhead, and the wind started picking up. Jane had no idea it was supposed to rain, so she didn't have an umbrella with her. It began to rain a misty kind of rain at first, like the haze of a dream, which seemed appropriate, because Jane felt like she was in a bad dream. She had no idea what happened to Ashley and Nate. *Why would they leave the museum without her, unless something bad had happened to them?* she thought to herself. Her only option was to return to the hotel.

The sky soon opened up and big cold drops of rain started pouring down. Jane could feel it running off her wet hair down her back and tried to adjust her hair to keep her shirt dry, to no avail. She saw a big flash of lightning that seemed close by and heard a boom of thunder. She passed some small shops and a bistro, where she could have ducked in to wait until the storm passed, but she had no time to waste finding out what happened to Ashley and Nate. Every time she thought about what might have happened to them, she stepped up her pace and walked as fast as she could.

Luckily, it was summer and it wasn't cold outside, although the soaking rain was making Jane shiver. It rained hard for about half of the distance back to the hotel, and Jane was completely drenched in a short time. She kept walking until she saw the sign for the hotel. She blinked and rubbed her eyes as she tried to read the sign, which was blurry in the haze of the rain. *Yes!* she thought to herself. *I made it to the hotel by myself! Well, with the help of my map app, but here I am. I hope Ashley and Nate are here.*

Jane pushed open the front door of the hotel and noticed the police were in the lobby. She tried to shake off some of the rain water just inside the door, and then she took the elevator up to their room. When she exited the elevator on their floor, Jane saw another policeman in the hallway talking to Ashley. The officer appeared to be taking notes. As she approached them, she could see that the door to their room was wide open.

"There you are!" she exclaimed. "I didn't know what happened to you back in the museum. I looked around and you were gone. What's going on?"

Ashley held up her index finger. "Just one sec," said Ashley, as she wrapped up her conversation with the officer. He went into their room.

"Ok," she said, "You and Nate disappeared in the museum, so I headed back here to the hotel. When I got to the room, a guy was running out the door and knocked into me. I found the maid lying on the floor and the room was trashed. It appears that someone was looking for something. Where were you guys?"

"Security grabbed me for taking a flash picture. And someone stole my wallet," Jane replied.

"Cancel your debit card right away," said Ashley. "I'm glad we left our passports back in the room safe, or I don't know how you'd get home. Wait – the safe!" Ashley went into the room and opened the safe. "Whew! Still there!"

"Do not touch anything," commanded one of the police officers.

"Sorry," said Ashley, as she held up her hands and walked back out into the hallway.

"Thanks Ash. Where's Nate? I thought he would be with you."

"He's not with me," said Ashley. "I couldn't find him either. You both just disappeared. He's not answering his cell phone."

"Oh," said Jane. "I don't know where to look for him. I guess we should wait here for him. When he can't find us, he'll find his way here eventually."

Jane called and canceled her card, while Ashley went into the room and continued chatting with the police. Two men came in with a stretcher and hauled out the maid. "Is she dead?" Ashley asked the policeman.

"Non(no), but very bad condition," he replied. "We will need your telephone number and photo identification, so that we may get in touch with you later."

"Sure," said Ashley. Is it okay to touch the safe now?" she asked.

"Oui," he replied.

Ashley opened the safe and took her passport out and handed it to him. "We will be in touch with you," he said, as he handed it back to her.

"Okay," replied Ashley.

After clearing the crime scene, the police left. Ashley surveyed the room from the open doorway. "What a mess," she said. The girls went back into the room, and Ashley put her passport back into the safe. Jane changed into some dry clothes and wrapped her wet hair in towel, while Ashley started to straighten up the room. They didn't have many belongings in the room, so it didn't take very long.

Ashley grabbed some granola and crackers off the

table and sat down on the bed. Jane took some cheese out of the refrigerator for the crackers and sat down with her. As they munched on their snacks, another half hour went by and the girls were getting worried.

"This is all my fault," said Jane. "We should have never come here. We should have just stayed home and stopped investigating things. Now we've lost Nate. What if something terrible happened to him? I'll never forgive myself," said Jane. She put her head in her hands.

Finally, Jane's cell phone rang – it was Nate. "Meet me at the entrance to the Eiffel tower as soon as you can get here," he said.

"Um, what's going on? Are you okay?" asked Jane.

"I'll tell you later. Just come meet me," he said and hung up.

"Okay," said Jane.

CHAPTER SIXTEEN

FROM BAD TO WORSE

THE GIRLS JUMPED up and headed out the door to the elevator. "I guess the quickest way to the Eiffel Tower is for us to run," said Ashley. "It's not far from the hotel. We can cut through the Parc du Champ de Mars."

"I'll do the best I can," said Jane, as they exited the elevator into the hotel lobby. "You know I'm not very fast… and I don't have my running shoes. Plus, it's raining."

"It looks like the rain is letting up," said Ashley, as she opened the front door of the hotel. She took off as soon as they stepped out onto the sidewalk. "C'mon, Jane!"

"I'm doing my best," Jane said, running about 10 feet behind Ashley. She was already panting hard before they reached the end of the block. Jane stopped a few times to catch her breath, while Ashley ran in circles around her until she was ready.

"Almost there," said Ashley, as they finally approached the Eiffel Tower. Jane did her best to catch up.

"Here's the entrance," said Ashley. "I don't see him."

Jane was out of breath. "I'll try calling him again," she said. She dug her phone out of her pocket and tried to call.

"There's no answer. He must be here somewhere," said Jane. The girls continued to search around the entrance for Nate for several minutes.

"I guess we should go back to the hotel again and see if he came back," said Ashley. They began walking back through the Parc du Champ de Mars to get to the hotel.

"What's that?" said Jane. "Are those shoes sticking out from behind that tree?"

"Where?" asked Ashley, looking around.

"Those look like Nate's shoes," said Jane, as she pointed towards the tree.

"Whoever that is, I hope they are just sleeping," said Ashley. The girls crept over to the tree to take a look. "It is Nate!" said Ashley.

"Nate, Nate, are you okay?" asked Jane, as she prodded his shoulder. He didn't move. She leaned down and cupped his face in her hands. "Nate! Oh God. It's my fault we came here," said Jane, tears streaming down her face.

"I encouraged it. I think I'm equally at fault," said Ashley.

Nate started to sit up with his hand on the back of his head. "Are you okay?" Jane repeated. Her tears began to subside.

"Just stupid, I guess," said Nate, as he held the back of his head and winced in pain.

"What in the world happened to you?" asked Ashley.

Nate sighed. "It's a long story."

"We want to hear all of it," said Ashley.

"Well… I saw that guy from the apartment at the museum. It looked like he lifted Jane's wallet out of her purse, so I followed him. There wasn't time to tell you where I was going."

"Did he follow us all morning?"

"I don't know," said Nate, "Maybe. He stopped at a coffee shop, so I waited outside until he came out. Then he headed over here. At some point, I think he must have realized he was being followed after I called you. After we got off the phone, I didn't see him. Then I turned to look for him and got hit in the back of the head with something. I don't know how I got over here."

"We need to take you to the hospital to make sure you're okay. You might have a concussion."

"I'm okay, really," he said.

"No, we're taking you," insisted Ashley. "An injury like that could be serious. Let's go," she said as she pulled him to his feet. With all of her years playing sports, Ashley knew a thing or two about injuries, especially concussions. And even though she was pretty easy going, when she made up her mind about something, it was hard to argue with her.

"Better safe than sorry," said Jane. She pulled out her cell phone and said, "What's the French word for hospital?"

"You'll have to look up the translation," said Ashley. "Search for the closest one."

"Here it is," said Jane. "l'hopital. There is the Hopital Georges Pompidou and Hopital Necker. Also, there's an American Hospital of Paris. I think we'd need to take the Métro and bus to that one, but they probably speak English there."

"Let's go to that one," said Ashley. "My French is not good at all. I don't even know how to say 'concussion' in French. I'm afraid we might not understand what they tell us, which isn't their problem, since we are in their country. But we need to be able to understand what they tell us."

"Wherever you pick is fine," said Nate, "but keep an eye out for the guy from the apartment. He's out here somewhere," said Nate, as he walked slowly. The girls each had an arm locked with his to steady him and keep him moving.

"Remember I have no money," said Jane.

"I have some Métro tickets in my backpack," said Ashley. "Let's head for the Métro. Jane, I'll hang onto Nate while you look up the nearest stop."

"Wait," said Jane. "It looks like there is a bus stop right here by Champ de Mars, and it will take a little over half hour to get there by bus."

"That works," said Ashley. "Lead the way," she said, as she locked her arm with Nate and pulled him forward towards Jane. They found the bus stop and waited there, keeping an eye out for the man from the apartment. Just as they were getting on the bus, a shot rang out. They all bolted up the stairs onto the bus. Jane and Ashley were dragging Nate.

"What was that?" said Jane. Ashley ducked down and peered out the bus window. "Get down," said Ashley, "and lay low. He doesn't know where we are getting off."

"I hope not," said Jane. "Keep an eye out to make sure he doesn't follow the bus."

Nate looked out the window and recognized the barefoot man from the apartment. He ducked down and the bus took off.

"O M G," said Jane. "What have we gotten ourselves into?"

Nate tried to doze off on the bus, but Ashley wouldn't let him. "Wake up tiger. No sleeping for you with a head injury."

"I think that's an old wive's tale," said Nate.

"Maybe, but that's what I always heard, so we're keeping you awake," said Ashley.

They arrived at the hospital and checked Nate in. He was shown to a room and checked out by the doctor on duty. They were all relieved that everyone spoke English to them. "You have don't have any concussion, symptoms, but you need to pay attention just in case," said the doctor. "You were lucky it wasn't more severe. Get your friend some sunglasses and follow this list of instructions," he told the girls. "If he experiences any of the symptoms on the list, he must follow the instructions.”

"We'll keep a close eye on him," promised Jane.

The doctor turned to Nate. "Take it easy for the next week."

"Thank you, doctor," said Nate. They took the bus back to the hotel to find the police waiting for them.

"We caught the man that was in the hotel room," said the policier (police officer). "It looks like the maid was not connected to him, but just came in to make the beds when he was ransacking the room. The desk clerk gave us an excellent description and we were able to pick him up. She also identified his photograph."

"I guess we were really lucky that we weren't in the room at the wrong time," said Ashley.

"Yes, you were very lucky," said the officer. "This man, Monsieur Dumont, is a known art thief that we have not been able to catch. He is part of a global art theft ring run by a man known as Pierre Moineau. We have been watching his house and have seen this man, Dumont, come and go. We need you to also identify him as the man you saw run out of the room. You will need to come to the commissariat de police."

"The what?" Ashley asked.

"The… police station," said the officer.

"Oh, okay, sure, I can do that," said Ashley. "Can you give me a ride there and back?"

"Oui (yes)," said the policier.

"You stay here and keep an eye on Nate, and I'll be right back," said Ashley. "Don't let him sleep yet."

"Okay," said Jane. "Be careful."

"Wait," said Jane. "We need to report that a man was shooting at us earlier when we were boarding a bus for the hospital. We were at the bus stop by Parc du Champ de Mars."

"Someone shot at you today?" asked the policier.

"Yes," said Jane.

"I had seen him earlier in the day at an apartment building. The name on the mailbox was Blanchet. Jane has the address," added Nate.

"About what time was that?" asked the policier.

"It was about two hours ago, I guess," said Nate. He looked at Jane.

"That sounds right," said Jane. She gave the address of the Blanchet apartment to the policier.

The policier turned to Ashley. "Did you also see this man that was shooting at you earlier?"

"Yes, I saw him."

"Good, then maybe you can also identify him from some photos. We can let the young man rest for now."

Ashley went to the police station to identify the man that she saw running out of their hotel room. "Yes, that's him," said Ashley. "I'm sure of it."

The police interrogated the man, named Dumont, to no avail. They finally had to make a deal for a lesser charge to motivate Dumont to surrender some useful information. He admitted that a man named Pierre Moineau paid him to go to their room and find out more about who they were. He was instructed to search the room and see if they had anything valuable.

He gave them enough information for a search warrant for Moineau's house. They looked up

Moineau in their database and found a photo of him. "Do you know this man?" the policier (police officer) asked Ashley.

"Yeah, that's the guy that shot at us when we were getting on the bus earlier today," she said. "I'd know him anywhere."

Meanwhile, Nate and Jane waited back in the hotel room. "No need to hover, Jane. Really, I'm okay," said Nate.

"I feel so bad about what happened to you," said Jane. "I can't believe that guy came after us. I had no idea."

"It's over and my head is sore, but otherwise I feel okay," said Nate, still holding ice on his head. "Can you get me some more ice?" he asked.

"Of course," said Jane. "Anything you need." Jane refilled Nate's ice pack with fresh ice out of the ice bucket.

"Thanks," said Nate. "Let's just stay safe until we get home."

"Deal," said Jane.

The police brought Ashley back to the hotel. "We may need you to return here for the trial for Monsieur Dumont, the man who attacked the hotel maid," said the policier, as Ashley got out of the car. "You are an important witness. We may also need you to testify regarding Monsieur Moineau firing shots at you and your friends."

"Uh, okay, I guess. I'll do whatever I can," said Ashley. "Thanks for the ride," she said. Ashley went back into the hotel and took the elevator back to the room.

Ashley returned to the hotel room to find Nate resting and Jane watching over him. "How's the patient?" she asked.

"I'm okay," said Nate.

"He still seems to be in a lot of pain," said Jane. "I'm so sorry I got you into this, Nate."

"It's not your fault I chose to follow him," said Nate. "I guess that wasn't a good idea. We should have never knocked on the door at that apartment, like I said, but I should also not have followed him from the museum."

"What happened at the police station?" asked Jane.

"I identified the guy they captured," said Ashley. "His name is Dumont. He gave up another guy named Moineau. He was the one that shot at us. I saw his picture. They are getting a search warrant for his house, based on the information from Dumont. I may need to come back and testify at the trial. They might want you two to testify about the guy that shot at us."

"I wouldn't mind coming back to Paris," said Jane. "But we'll absolutely have to stay out of trouble next time."

"Wasn't that the plan this time?" asked Nate.

"Um, yeah," said Jane.

The next morning, the trio woke up at 3:30 AM again. They packed up their backpacks and checked out of the hotel. Sitting in the lobby waiting for the taxi to pick them up, Jane felt her butterflies churning again. She was anxious to get to the airport before something else happened. *Hopefully at this hour of the morning, no one will see us*, she thought.

The taxi picked them up and they arrived at Paris Charles deGaulle airport on time. They checked in for their flight and sat down to wait for boarding. "I'm so ready to go home," said Jane. "This was an amazing adventure. I can't believe we've only been here a couple of days."

"I know, right?" said Ashley. "It seems like it was much longer."

"Next time I want to visit the Eiffel Tower," said Jane.

CHAPTER SEVENTEEN

HOME SWEET HOME

THE PLANE TOOK off for the long flight home. Jane looked somberly out the window at the Paris skyline and wondered if she'd ever get to come back and see the rest of the city. It was a whirlwind few days, and Jane had mixed feelings about her time here.

Her fleeting experience in Paris created so many images throughout her mind, that it would take her a while to sort them all out. She enjoyed seeing the city, trying new foods, spending time at the park and seeing some of the sites. However, she didn't enjoy the part where her wallet was stolen, Nate was attacked, and a man shot at them getting on the bus. For those reasons, she was happy to be headed home for now.

After a layover in New York, the trio boarded their flight for the last leg of their trip back to Ohio. Jane slept most of the way. They were relieved to arrive at the West Midland airport without another incident.

After loading their backpacks in Bernice, they headed to Ashley's parents' house to pick up Edward. Ashley didn't want to waste another minute being separated from her best pal.

Edward leaped up in the backseat to sit by Nate. "Hi there, boy, good to see you," he said, as Edward licked his face and hands. He wiped his hands on his jeans.

"Your house is next, Nate," said Jane.

"And just in time," said Nate. "I have to work in the morning."

"And I need to get to the gym in the morning," said Ashley. "I know it's been just a few days, but it seems like forever."

"I'm happy to be home but I really miss my grandparents. They were only supposed to be gone for two weeks and I haven't heard anything at all about whether they are okay. I don't know why I thought going to Paris was gonna help them at all. I feel helpless. There's nothing I can do for them, and no one is telling me anything."

"Don't give up Jane," said Ashley. "They would never give up on you. You need to hang onto the hope that they are okay until you have undeniable proof that they are not."

"Thanks, Ash. I needed to hear that. I just feel like I should be there for them, and do something, but I just don't know what to do. They are everything to me. I can't lose them."

Nate chimed in. "You've done everything you can do. Just keep the faith and take care of the house for them. I know how hard this must be for you."

"Thanks, Nate. What about that painting? How can the same painting be in the Musée d'Orsay and in my grandparents' house?"

"Yeah, it doesn't make sense," said Ashley. "One of them must not be real or maybe the artist painted more than one?"

"Now that is a mystery that I can't explain," said Nate. "The same painting in two places? I was thinking about what I can find out at the library when I get back there."

"I hope you can find something, but you've already gone above and beyond trying to help solve this mystery," said Jane. "You don't have to keep looking."

"No, it's fun! I really want to solve it," said Nate.

"Okay then, if you want," Jane replied.

"There's my house," said Nate. "The fourth one on the left with the blue shutters. Thanks."

"You keep an eye on that head injury," said Ashley. "Don't be a hero, take care of it like the doc told you."

"I promise I will," said Nate. "I feel okay, though." He grabbed his backpack and patted Edward on the head, before closing the backdoor of Bernice.

Jane, Ashley, and Edward headed home. Jane navigated down the long driveway to the back of her grandparents' house. Edward went first in the back door, with Ashley and Jane following. He sniffed around and the house seemed quiet. Ashley surveyed the rooms and reported that all was well. Jane breathed in the sweet smell of vanilla and sighed happily.

Jane plopped down in one of the chairs by the fireplace. She thought she was going to relax the rest of the day.

"Back to normal," announced Ashley. "We have the rest of the day free. Time for a run!"

"Seriously?"

"You know we all need it, Jane. Get your running gear on."

"Okay," said Jane. "Give me 15 minutes."

"Fifteen minutes counting down. Starting now," said Ashley, pretending to look at a watch on her wrist.

Jane went back to her bedroom to change into her shorts and running shoes. She looked over at her mom's picture on the dresser. "Thanks for watching over us, Mom," she said as she blew her mom's picture a kiss.

"Okay, I'm ready," said Jane, coming down the hallway. "Why are we in a hurry to do this?"

"Because," said Ashley. "We can't let ourselves get down. We have to keep moving forward. When we can't move forward in other ways, we can always run or do something to physically move forward."

Ashley hooked Edward's leash to his collar and opened the back door. He ran out excitedly and leaped around in the driveway, while Jane locked the back door. "Off we go," said Ashley, after they stretched a bit in the driveway. Edward led the way as fast as Ashley would let him run. Ashley started out slowly again so Jane could keep up.

"Hey," said Ashley. "I think you're a little faster

this time.”

“I feel like it’s slightly easier,” said Jane, already panting. “I’m not saying it’s easy, though. But I remember how it felt when we were finished last time. It was amazing. I think I could learn to get better at this. It always makes me so happy to be outdoors.”

Ashley led Jane and Edward around the neighborhood for a mile, before they turned around and headed back to the house. Jane was panting hard, but hanging in there. “Let’s stretch a little bit before we go in,” said Ashley.

“Okay,” said Jane. She was sweating and panting, and was relieved they were finished running.

“That was two miles again!” Ashley smiled. “Good work, Jane. I knew you could do it.”

“Still not very fast, though,” said Jane, still out of breath.

“That’s not the point,” said Ashley. “And you’ll get faster.”

Edward was the first one in the door. He went to his bowl and pushed it with his nose. “Sorry boy, I’ll fill that,” said Ashley. She filled the bowl with water and Edward immediately started slurping it up. Jane filled two water glasses and handed one to Ashley. Jane leaned against the counter and started drinking the other one.

“You’re right,” said Jane. “That wore me out, but it did make me feel a lot better.”

“I knew it would,” said Ashley.

“I have another graduation party tonight,” said Jane. “Do you have anything going on?”

"Nope, Edward and I will guard the house this evening," said Ashley. "I'm going to the gym first, though."

CHAPTER EIGHTEEN
A SURPRISE FOR JANE

THE NEXT MORNING, Jane and Peaches met some friends at the school courts to play tennis for fun. She loved tennis even more with friends, as it gave them something to do together while practicing their game skills, with no pressure. It felt like forever since she had played, even though it wasn't.

It was getting close to lunchtime when they were finished playing. Peaches and Jane walked to the parking lot together.

"Have you decided whether to go to West Midland U?" asked Jane.

"Yes, it makes sense for me to go there. And since my father is a professor at the school, he is all for it, of course. No pressure there, ya know?" Peaches laughed.

"That's great!" said Jane. "I would really miss you if we went to different colleges."

"Yeah, me too," said Peaches. "But I won't be at orientation. My family will be on vacation that week."

"Well, I'll be going, so I can tell you if there's anything important that you missed," said Jane.

"That's cool," said Peaches. "Thanks."

Jane headed home in Bernice. When she pulled down the long driveway to the back of the house, Jane spotted her dad's car in the driveway. Her face lit up with a smile. *Dad's back!* she thought to herself.

She hurried out of the car and through the back door. "Dad? Ash?"

"In here, Pumpkin," called Dad from the living room. Jane dropped her tennis bag by the door and rushed into the room to see her dad. She couldn't believe what she was seeing.

"Grandma! Grandpa!" she exclaimed. "I can't believe my eyes! I knew you couldn't be dead." Tears were streaming down Jane's face as she hugged them both as tightly as she could.

"Yes, dear, we are finally home," said Grandma. Her grandparents both gave Jane a big hug, while Edward joined the group by licking her hands and wagging his tail.

"It's so good to see you, my dear," said Grandma. "Your dad has been filling us in on what has gone on while we were away. I must say, you've had quite a busy summer, helping the authorities round up all of those criminals!"

"Summer was nothing like I expected," said Jane. "That's for sure. What in the world happened on your cruise?" asked Jane.

"That's a long story," said Grandpa. "But we'll tell you all about it."

"I can't wait to hear this," said Ashley. Ashley leaned back in the chair. Edward barked once in agreement and then settled down by Ashley's feet.

"I guess it all started about ten years ago, when your grandma and I were still in the Army. The government had seized two paintings from an auction in France that were identified as stolen in the Art Loss Register. This is a global database that includes listings of artworks that have been lost or stolen over many decades, whether through the Nazi seizures during World War II or other means."

"I learned about that database from my friend, Nate, at the library," said Jane, nodding her head.

"Your grandma and I both worked for the Office of Civil Affairs in the Army, as I think you know. The U.S. and France were cooperating with the Belgian government to return these two paintings to the families that had originally owned them, before Nazi Germany invaded the country in 1940. They had been missing for many decades. One was called Boat in Wind, and the other one was Blue Garden. Both were painted by Rémy Destombes, a Belgian painter from the 1700s."

Grandpa continued his story. "The man who put the items up for sale in the auction was the head of a global art theft ring. He had a false identity that he had built through nefarious means. He had purchased a magnificent house in Paris, a Rolls Royce, and was hobnobbing with the most affluent people in Europe.

Everyone believed he was on the up and up. He even made large donations to charitable organizations, leading everyone to believe he was an honest man, and also a philanthropist."

"When did you say all this happened?" asked Jane.

"This was about ten years ago," said Grandpa. "It was a gallery dealer that first questioned the paintings, then another dealer thought the same thing. When the two paintings in the auction were discovered to be stolen, it all started to fall apart. They asked your grandma to take a look at them and she verified that the two paintings were the stolen original works. They also brought in the FBI to work with them and do some investigating into his other dealings."

"Wow, Grandma. I had no idea that you used to do that until recently," said Jane.

Grandpa continued, "Before they could arrest him, he went into hiding. He knew he was facing a lengthy prison sentence if he was caught. He's been on the run all this time — for almost ten years. His name is Pierre Moineau."

"Moineau! That was the name of the barefoot man from the apartment in Paris!" said Jane. "This is the same man that was hiding for ten years?"

"Yes, Pierre Moineau is the man they just captured," said Grandma. "The reason we went on the cruise is related to an incident that occurred about six months ago. There is an apartment in Paris that was recently discovered to have a trove of paintings that were stolen during World War II, that had been hidden and passed down from father to daughter. The father was in Hitler's army and had helped loot art works for the Nazis from families in several countries during World War II. He had saved some precious items for himself, without Hitler's knowledge."

"I guess you can't trust anyone, can you?" Jane smirked.

"When he died," Grandma continued, "he left the apartment where he had been living since the war to his daughter, Charmaine. Charmaine Blanchet has been living in this apartment in Paris all of these years with this hidden collection of stolen paintings."

"Blanchet!" said Jane. "That's the name on the mailbox of the apartment we saw in Paris."

"Yes, Blanchet," said Grandpa. "I don't know why you would have been there, but Charmaine Blanchet had these stolen paintings in that apartment for decades, and no one knew about them."

"What did this apartment full of stolen paintings have to do with Grandma?" asked Jane.

Grandpa continued, "We were told that one day when Charmaine had the door open to get the newspaper, a neighbor spotted a familiar painting from the hallway and got suspicious and reported her. The neighbor thought she had seen it in an old photo of her grandparents. The investigation became the responsibility of the government and the Civil Affairs office became involved. Your grandmother's expertise was requested from the Civil Affairs office, even though she was already retired. They just wanted her to take a quick trip to Paris to help them verify some of the paintings. There were so many of them that they wanted additional assistance from her, if she was available."

"Oh, when you two went to Paris last winter?" asked Jane.

"Yes," said Grandpa.

"I thought you went for fun," said Jane.

"We did have a little time to do some sightseeing on that trip, and enjoyed a few delicious meals in Paris. However, it was the Army's request that prompted it," said Grandpa.

"When we were leaving Charmaine Blanchet's apartment, we saw Pierre Moineau on the street out in front. Your grandma was absolutely sure it was him. They locked eyes for a moment and she was sure he recognized her, as well. So, we let the authorities know. That gave them a starting point for his current location, but it wasn't easy tracking him down. It took months, but they learned more about his more recent transactions, which he had been doing through other people. One of the people he worked with was Sheila Radford, whom I understand you recently met."

"Oh… yes. We met." said Jane, feeling a little uneasy. "So Moineau and Sheila were working together?"

"Yes, it seems they were. We learned that Sheila was selling stolen works through Moineau," said Grandpa.

"Just before your graduation, the Army officer in charge of the investigation told us that we needed to disappear for a few weeks and suggested we take this cruise," said Grandma. "They didn't say for sure that we were in any danger, but said they had some reliable information that someone was looking for us, someone that had been hired by Pierre Moineau. They didn't want us to take any chances."

"When they still hadn't arrested Pierre, they thought it might lead this person to the cruise ship and when that didn't work, they thought it might bring this person out into the open if we were presumed dead, so an explosion was staged on the cruise. They made sure that only the local news in Paris carried the story, so that Moineau would hear it, and you would not hear about it."

"But someone told Dad about it," said Jane.

"That wasn't supposed to happen," said Grandpa. "I'm so sorry you had to worry about us. We thought the less you knew, the better. We had hoped to get all of this drama wrapped up without involving or disrupting your life any more than necessary. Your father didn't know either, but one of his contacts in France unexpectedly alerted him about the explosion. We couldn't tell anyone."

"I do wish the Army had communicated this to us earlier and given us the complete scenario," said Jane's dad. "I only had part of the story of what was going on. But in our business, everyone is on a need-to-know basis. My partner, Jim, and I already had the house under surveillance 24 hours a day watching Bob's activities, but then the Army did alert us to the possibility that someone had been hired to come after your grandparents. Sure enough, as it turns out, a known assassin started hanging close to the house."

"An assassin?" asked Jane, exchanging surprised looks with Ashley.

Jane's dad continued. "Moineau wanted to make sure your grandparents would not to be able to testify against him. They were not after you, but I couldn't have been happier when you and Ashley made a timely decision to go to Paris for a few days. I thought you'd be safer there. Once we knew who he had sent here, we were able to track her communication and our French counterparts intercepted the calls with Moineau and gathered the evidence we needed to take her in. I certainly did not expect for you to be anywhere near him or have any interaction with him, but he is now in custody, and so is the assassin."

"Her?" asked Jane.

"Yes. It was a woman. She was arrested in her hotel room, just outside of West Midland, along with a long-range rifle with a scope and a large amount of cash. A man named Dumont provided the location of Moineau's house in Paris."

"Who is she? The assassin, I mean," said Jane. "I didn't know anyone was out there," she said, looking at Ashley. Ashley shrugged her shoulders.

"She didn't have to be close by to do the job she was hired to do," said Grandpa. "Her long-range rifle allowed her to be pretty far away from the house, farther than even Edward could sense. But she was masquerading at some points as a real estate agent, in order to snoop around."

"A real estate agent?" said Jane, with raised eyebrows.

"Yes, her name was," said Grandpa. He looked at Grandma and tapped his forehead as he tried to think of her name.

"Angela Mott," said Grandma. "That's the name she was using. Her real name is Stephanie Holmes."

"Yes, yes, that's correct," said Grandpa.

"We saw her talking to Bob in the driveway, so we were keeping an eye on her anyway. She came to the door a few times," said Jane's dad, "but Edward sent her away pretty quickly. Right?"

"That's right!" said Ashley. "I can't believe she was an assassin! I thought she was Barbie's sister! "

"People can appear any way they want," said Dad. "That's what makes it so difficult to look at someone and know what they are up to. It's never obvious when working with criminals."

"Stephanie is suspected for two other recent hits. I'm not sure if they are related to Moineau or not. But the FBI is holding her for questioning while they investigate," said Dad.

"So, let me get this straight," said Ashley. "You were all working together this whole time?"

"No, actually we weren't," said Grandma. "Your Uncle Bill had worked in a different department in the FBI, before he took a job with West Midland Security for several years to be closer to home for Jane after your aunt died. We never worked with him when Grandpa and I were in the Army. Grandpa was in a different department in our unit than I was. He worked on a civil reconnaissance team."

She turned to Jane. "But when your dad recently

went back to the FBI, when he had to move to be closer to Washington D.C., he went to the art theft unit. He knew a bit about my artwork collection and expertise, and when a position opened up, he applied for it. He thought it was interesting work, and shared my passion for getting the families and their valuable items reunited. Paintings, vases, and other items were important to these families and a large part of their family history. It was just devastating what happened when these items were ravaged back during the war. Even the Mona Lisa was missing for a period of time – stolen right out of a museum!"

"I heard about that!" said Jane. Edward started barking.

Just then the doorbell rang. "Who could that be?" asked Jane. "I hope Angela AKA Stephanie isn't back."

"I'll get it," offered Jane's dad, as he got up and headed to the door. Edward followed him.

"Come on in," Jane heard him say. "It's okay, Edward," said Jane's dad, as he patted Edward on the head.

Jane looked up, and there was the man with the monster truck tee shirt that she had seen on several occasions in parking lots. *Was this Brandi Brown's brother from the school parking lot?* she wondered to herself.

Edward was sniffing him and licking his hand. *It looks like Edward approves*, thought Jane.

"Everyone, this is my partner, Jim," said Jane's dad. "If you remember, Jane and Ashley, he was injured in our encounter with Bob, but he's doing much better now."

Jane smiled. She remembered the role Jim played in protecting her from Bob. "Nice to meet you Jim, I'm Jane." Jane stepped forward and held out her hand to shake his hand. Her dad smiled, as he thought that was just like her mom used to do. Jane's mom was always bold when meeting new people. He had not seen that confidence from Jane before now.

"I've seen you around," said Jane, "but had no idea who you were. You're not wearing your monster truck shirt today. I'm glad to know you're one of the good guys."

"Thanks," chuckled Jim. "You're not easy to keep up with," said Jim. He winked at Jane.

"Oh?" said Jane. "Ohhhh... that was you across the street from the apartment in Paris, wasn't it? I wasn't sure."

"No, that wasn't me. That was my French counterpart, Franck Giraud, that was keeping an eye on Charmaine Blanchet's apartment building. What were you doing there?"

"Well, er … Ashley and I were cleaning the house, like Dad asked us to do." She turned to look at her dad. "And I found a key under the clock on the mantel while I was dusting. We didn't know if Grandma and Grandpa were in trouble, and thought it might lead to a clue to help them. We thought it seemed odd that they would hide it somewhere that it would be so easily found."

"You found the key to the desk?" asked Grandpa.

"Yes," said Jane. "Remember at the time we didn't know if you and Grandma were dead or alive. I was scared and wanted to help, so I looked around until I found that it fit the desk. I looked in the log book and saw the Paris address on it, and wondered what was there. I thought it might lead to a clue to find out what happened to you, and I guess it sorta did," said Jane, with tears in her eyes. "I realize now that it was a dumb thing to do."

"I'm sorry, Dad," said Jane. She turned to her dad and gave him a hug.

Jane's dad sighed. He understood what Jane was thinking at the time. "Don't do anything like that again. No more investigating," said her dad.

"You're my family," said Jane. "I'd do anything for you."

Jim interrupted. "My counterpart in Paris, Franck, saw Moineau bump into you at the Louvre and walk away with your wallet," said Jim. "You really shouldn't walk around Paris with a purse out in the open. I'm surprised no one warned you about that."

"Actually, the hotel manager did. We left our backpacks and passports in the room," said Jane. "I didn't think a small purse would be a problem. I guess I was wrong."

Jim continued. "In this case, Moineau followed you when you were sniffing around the Blanchet apartment, and Franck was following him. I guess Moineau wanted to know who you were, so he lifted the wallet to get to your identification. Pierre, in turn, contacted Dumont to search your hotel room. Your room key inside the wallet provided the information he needed, and he would have been able to tell from your name and address on your driver's license that you lived at your grandparents' house. You really put yourself in danger when you two and your friend went to Paris, but it helped smoke him out of hiding where we could find him."

Jane's dad turned to look at both girls. "You don't know how dangerous it can be to knock on the wrong door," said Jane's dad. "But once we had Moineau and Stephanie Holmes in custody, it was safe for your grandparents to finally come home."

"Eventually, you should be able to get your wallet back, but it is still being held in Paris as evidence. It was found in Moineau's house during the search. It could take a while. You should go ahead and get a new ID and whatever else was in there," advised Jim.

"Thanks, Jim, for all the information. Finally, all the pieces are starting to fit together in this puzzle. Please let Franck know I appreciate all he's done," said Jane.

"Jim, Bill, would you like to join us for lunch?" said Grandma.

"I hate to run, but we can't stay," said Jane's dad, "Jim and I have to get back to DC for some follow-up meetings. Now we get to do all the paperwork to wrap up this investigation."

"Ashley, again, thank you for being here for Jane, and thank you too, Edward. He really is a great dog, you know," said Dad. "Aren't you boy?" Edward wagged his tail as soon as he heard his name.

"I sure do," beamed Ashley.

CHAPTER NINETEEN

A NEW PHASE BEGINS

THE NEXT MORNING, Ashley and Jane sat down to breakfast with Jane's grandparents. Breakfast always started with a half of a grapefruit with Grandma, no matter what else you were having to eat. Luckily, Jane loved grapefruit.

Jane smiled as she looked around. She was happy that the people she cared most about, other than her dad, were okay and were sitting around the breakfast table with her.

"How's Bernice holding up?" asked Grandpa. "I heard you drove her to New York."

"Great," said Jane. "Thanks for taking such good care of her. She drove like a dream. Parking in New York was pretty expensive though. I understand why some people that live there don't even own cars. It's pretty easy to get around without one, once you're there."

"You accomplished quite a bit this summer," said Grandpa. "Most kids just spend the summer having fun."

"I'm glad you think that, Grandpa," said Jane. "It was a little frightening at times, but Ashley and Nate were the best support I could have. I don't know what I'd do without them."

"The three of you, and Edward, helped round up several criminals. You put yourself in danger, and I wish you wouldn't have, but I understand why," said Grandpa.

"I'm just so relieved you and Grandma are safely home," said Jane.

"The house looks pretty clean," said Grandma. "It looks like you girls took good care of it while we were gone."

"We sure tried," said Ashley.

"When will we meet Nate?" asked Grandma.

"Soon," said Jane. "I can't wait for you and Grandpa to meet him."

After breakfast, Ashley packed up her stuff and set it by the back door. "It's been great having you here, Ash. I don't know what I would have done without you and Edward this summer," said Jane. "I can always count on you."

"Of course, you can, little cousin," said Ashley. "I enjoyed it, too. I mean, my parents are great, but it was cool to stay here with you, and do a little sleuthing. And our trip to Paris was awesome. I hope we can go back just to see more of it."

"It was," said Jane. "I had fun... you know... for

the fun part of it!"

Ashley grabbed her bags and Edward's leash from beside the door. "C'mon Edward!" she said, as she held the door open. Edward ran out the door and hopped into the seat of Ashley's Jeep. Ashley followed him out. "Bye Jane!"

"Bye," said Jane as she closed the back door. Jane sat down on the sofa in the living room. She listened to the whir of the dome clock on the mantel and thought about all that had gone on this summer. Her grandparents were home, and everything was back to normal. She wasn't sure it ever would be normal again, but now it was.

Jane turned her attention to college. Tomorrow, she would visit the college campus for orientation, and sign up for her classes, and it wouldn't be long before school would begin.

The next day, Jane drove Bernice to the West Midland University campus. She had driven past the campus many times before now, but this was her first time to actually visit and walk around. Grandpa had offered to come with her, but Jane decided she felt comfortable exploring on her own. She thought Rachel might be here today, but hadn't talked to her in a while.

Jane found the appropriate parking lot and parked Bernice. As she walked the paved pathway towards the buildings, she noticed all the shade trees and benches scattered around a grassy area. *This seems so much better than the high school campus*, she thought. She could picture herself sitting outside eating her lunch and talking to friends in between classes.

Jane followed the signs to the introductory meeting for the orientation at one of the lecture halls. She soon was disappointed when she spotted Brandi Brown. *Another four years of her? Ugh, why can't she go to a different college?* she thought. Out of habit, Jane stepped through the crowd away from where Brandi was standing. She sat in the back corner farthest away from Brandi.

At the end of the session, Jane was one of the first ones out the door. She was walking towards the commons area to get something to drink, when Brandi spotted Jane and ran towards her. "Jane, Jane!"

What in the world could she want? thought Jane. *And what's she doing here without her besties? This seems different.*

"Let's sit down over here," said Brandi, pointing to a bench. Jane sighed and sat down on the bench with Brandi.

"Okay, but not for long," she said. "I have to be somewhere in a few minutes."

"I've had the worst summer," Brandi complained. "My mother became ill right after graduation, and it's been really hard. Heather and Brittany are nowhere to be found. I thought they were my friends, but they don't want to hear about it, or even hang out anymore. They don't even answer my calls. I can't just take off and go places with them when my mother is sick and needs me. Can I?"

"No, you're right," said Jane. "If your mother needs you, then that's where you should be. Don't worry about them. If they are your real friends, you'll know it."

"Real friends?" said Brandi. "What do you mean?"

"Real friends are there for each other, so you'll know if you think they are there for you or not," said Jane, not drawing any conclusions.

"Oh, I guess," said Brandi, looking puzzled.

"How is your mother doing now?" asked Jane.

"Oh, she is about the same," said Brandi. "A little better, I guess."

"Well, I hope she continues to improve," said Jane.

"Thanks." Brandi smiled at Jane. "I saw the roster for the tennis team, but I didn't see you on it," said Brandi. "Heather and Brittany aren't going to college here, and I didn't see anyone on it whose name I recognize. You are joining the team, aren't you?" she asked.

"Brandi, I'm surprised you are asking me that," replied Jane.

"You're surprised? But you were on the high school team," she said.

"I know, but you didn't want me to be on the team," said Jane. "I don't want to go through that again."

"Oh," said Brandi. She sat there for a minute without saying anything. "I guess it might not have been so fun for you, huh?" said Brandi thoughtfully.

"No. It could have been, if you were nicer," said Jane, surprised at herself for saying that out loud. "Like I said, I'm not going through it again," said Jane. She tried not to say more than necessary to get her point across.

"I'm sorry, Jane. I guess I was competing with you," admitted Brandi, as she looked down at the ground.

"Competing with me? Why?" said Jane, with a puzzled look. "We were on the same team."

"I know," said Brandi. She looked back up at Jane. "I don't know why I felt that way. Please sign up for the college team. I don't want to be on it alone."

"I will think about it," said Jane. "That's all I can promise."

"You need to sign up by the end of the week," said Brandi. "I feel like it's been a long summer and that high school was a long time ago. I hope we can put it behind us."

"I hope so too," said Jane. "I have to go," she said as she got up to leave. "See ya."

"Bye," said Brandi, as she continued to sit on the bench by herself.

Jane headed for commons area again when she spotted Rachel. "Rachel!" Jane shouted.

Rachel stopped and looked. She waved at Jane. "Jane!" Jane caught up with Rachel and started walking with her.

"I missed you this summer!" said Rachel. "I hope you're doing okay. We need to catch up."

"Yes, let's have lunch or something as soon as orientation weekend is over."

"Sounds great," said Rachel.

Jane and Rachel walked to the commons area together to get something to drink. There were tables set up with clubs and activities to join. Jane wasn't sure what she wanted to do, so she gathered information for several different activities.

After a long day of orientation sessions, Jane couldn't wait to get home and visit with her grandparents.

"I'm back," called Jane, as she opened the back door of the house.

"In here," said Grandma from the living room. "How was orientation?"

"It was good, I guess," said Jane. I saw some people from high school that will be going there, too."

"Oh?" said Grandma.

"Of course, I already know Peaches will be attending, but she wasn't at orientation. I saw my friend Rachel there, and she'll be going this year, too, which I'm happy about. I also saw Brandi Brown. I'm sure you remember her. I was hoping she would go somewhere else, but she seems to have had a tough summer. Maybe she won't be the same, which would be a good thing."

"How so?" asked Grandma.

"Well, her mom has been sick, and it sounds like the people she thought were her friends have ditched her. She was saying she hoped I would join the tennis team, which really surprised me."

"Why were you surprised?"

"Because she's been so mean to me. However, today she was being nice, and even before that she didn't really bother me. I feel like there's no reason to let someone like her bother me after everything that happened this summer. She didn't seem to realize how she came across. She seemed a little surprised when I told her."

"Well, that sounds promising," said Grandma. "Maybe it won't be a problem to be at the same school another four years."

"Yeah, I don't think it will be. I tried to avoid her, but when I couldn't, I realized I didn't feel the same way anymore. Even if she gets some new friends, I sort of see her differently now. I feel like a lot has changed. I kind of feel sorry for her. She seems kind of lost."

"Are you going to join the tennis team?" asked Grandma.

"I might," said Jane. "I don't think it matters to me anymore whether Brandi is on it, and I know that she did sign up. I am thinking about it."

"Well, good," said Grandma. "I wouldn't want that girl to keep you from doing something you love."

"I wouldn't either," said Jane.

"Grandma," said Jane. "There's something I need to tell you."

"Oh?" said Grandma.

"After the police left … you know … when I found Bob in the living room dead, there was a big mess to clean up. I started putting things back on the shelf when I discovered the bookcase opened and that there was a secret room.

"Oh, dear," said Grandma, "you found the room." Grandma chuckled. "There was a lot of history in that room at one time. We were storing some paintings in there that were being returned to their rightful owners," Grandma explained.

"But there is still one in there," says Jane.

"Oh yes," said Grandma. "The real one is in the Musée d'Orsay in Paris. That one in the room is a forgery and the owner was angry to find that out. He had paid a lot of money for it. As it turns out, it was actually painted in New York by an immigrant from Tunisia for a small amount of cash. It's not really valuable since it was forged."

"Why do you still have it?" asked Jane.

"For a while, we were holding it as evidence against an art thief," said Grandma. "But by the time the trial was completed, the owner had died and had no family, and it's been sitting there ever since. I'm not sure exactly what I should do with it. I've checked about donating it to a museum, but they are only interested in the original one. The original one was painted by a man named Gaston Brochard."

"How can you tell the difference?" Jane asked. "They look exactly alike. I saw the Brochard painting in the museum in Paris."

"You did? Oh, there are ways to tell," said Grandma. "You have to be able to understand the artists and the materials, as well as where the artist lived, what they painted, and what materials were available to them. People usually forge oil paintings, as watercolors are much more difficult to control. It's quite a lucrative, although illegal, business, as art can hold values in the millions of dollars.

"It sounds like a lot of knowledge is required for all

those details," said Jane.

"Yes, there is. If a painting is supposed to be created in a certain year, then all the materials used in the painting had to be available at that time and in that place," Grandma continued. "Artists were also limited in the materials used in the painting and their methods, so if an artist was copied, it had to be believable that this artist could have painted this painting."

"That sounds complicated," said Jane.

"I guess it is," replied Grandma. "The forger has to do a lot of things correctly to fool the experts. This artist used a type of paint that was not available in the year it was supposed to have been created. It wasn't available until over 50 years later. So, it was obvious this painting was a forgery. One wrong detail can point to a forgery, so the forger has to be very careful in order to get away with it."

"Wow, that's amazing," said Jane. "You could tell just by a type of paint being used that it was a forgery."

"That's right," said Grandma. "Brochard's original paintings are quite valuable, so the owner was duped out of a large amount of money for that forgery."

"That seems really unfair," said Jane. "I would have been angry, too."

"It makes me feel good when I can prevent that from happening. It's been such a joy to learn everything I can in this field, and there is still so much more to know. Experts sometimes disagree, until one of them points out a nuance they noticed that verifies the forgery or that authenticates a painting. I wish I could pass on everything I've learned."

"I've missed you and Grandpa so much this summer," said Jane. "But I've learned more about you both than I ever knew before… and Dad, too. Now I miss Ashley and Edward, since they went back to Ashley's parents' house. I was so used to having them here. It's been a strange summer. I don't quite feel like the same person, but maybe that's a good thing."

"It's always a good thing when we have our family together and we've grown as individual people," said Grandma, as she gave Jane a hug. "You've had quite a summer."

***

Review Request

Thank you for taking the time to read this book. I hope you enjoyed it and found the story to be entertaining.

I would love to have your feedback, and would be grateful if you would post an honest review of the book. I enjoy learning more about the reader's point of view. Your support and feedback does make a difference.

1. To leave a review, please visit ***The Secret Behind the Bookcase*** book page on Amazon.com.
2. Scroll down to the ***Customer Reviews*** section.
3. Locate the button labeled ***Write a customer review*** and click the button to enter your review.

Thank you in advance for your feedback! Look for Jane's second adventure, ***The Mystery on Snake Mountain***, on Amazon.com or check your local bookstore.

For further information, please contact the author at: info@hundredacrepress.com.
Or snail mail to:
Hundred Acre Press LLC
P.O. Box 54316
Cincinnati, OH 45254